MURDERED BY THE MIST

DERRICK MALLOW MYSTERIES
BOOK 2

J.L. MELTON

Published 2024 by Next Chapter

Cover art by Jaylord Bonnit

This book is dedicated to my friends and family

CHAPTER 1

Summertime is here in Lake Tisdale. This is the peak tourist season in Jenkins County. All the hotels, motels, and bed and breakfast accommodations are at full capacity.

This is when the population of Lake Tisdale grows by thousands.

It is Friday morning, June 20, 2025, and the first day of summer. It began with a thick gray mist hovering over the lake, the town, and most of Jenkins County.

At Toby's Bakery and Coffee Shop are the entire Lake Tisdale police force, including the new Homicide Investigations Department detectives led by Derrick Mallow.

The bakery and coffee shop are busy this morning, with the regular crowd and the vacationing tourists.

The law enforcement officers are sitting at their favorite table in the corner: Chief Adams and his wife Alice, Derrick Mallow and Greta McCall, Lucinda Brooks, Gail Stephens, Mason Briggs, Martin and Angela Taylor, and Franklin Stokes. They are having breakfast and morning conversation.

"I am glad we were all able to get together this morning. We can enjoy a great breakfast and talk about the first official day of the new Homicide Investigations Department, which begins Monday morning," the chief said happily.

"And I am glad that Toby finally decided to serve grits, eggs, bacon, sausage, toast, and hash browns for breakfast. It's a good change from doughnuts and pastries," Franklin said, stuffing his face with bacon.

"Greta, you like the lake so far?" Lucinda asked curiously while buttering her toast.

"It's a beautiful place. I am looking forward to working with all of you and living here for a long time," Greta said sincerely.

"Chief, when do we get the other six police officers?" Assistant Chief Mason Briggs asked while pouring more coffee into his cup.

"The interviews are completed, and the mayor and I will have to decide on the six best applicants out of nearly a hundred."

"DM, you eager to get started as the head of detectives next week?" Martin asked while watching the reaction of Mallow and the others.

"Martin, I am eager as I am going to get. I feel we will do a good job, and hopefully, keep our beautiful town, lake, and county safe," Mallow said as he looked at Greta and smiled.

"I know we will finally be able to keep our town safe for the good people of Lake Tisdale," the chief said, smiling and taking a swallow of coffee.

"Did y'all see how thick that mist was this morning? I could barely see the road," Greta said.

"Yes, I noticed that *too*, Greta. I have never seen it that *dense* before," Alice said as she wiped her mouth with a napkin.

"Now that y'all mentioned it. It was denser than usual this time of year," Lucinda said as she got up to pick out a couple of doughnuts from the 'sweets counter.'

"So, it is not usually this dense in the mornings?" Greta asked curiously as she watched two sheriff deputy cruisers park in front of the bakery and coffee shop.

"Derrick, is that Jim Matthews in one of those cruisers?" Greta asked as she watched Deputy Matthews and two other deputies enter.

"I believe it is, Greta."

Jim Matthews saw the chief, Mallow, and the others, then he quickly approached their table holding his gloves in his right hand.

"Good morning, chief, Derrick, Greta, Martin, Mason, Lucinda, Angela, Franklin, and Mrs. Adams, how are y'all doing?" Deputy Matthews said politely.

"I would like to introduce two new additions to the sheriff's department. This is Deputy Susan Davis, and this tall gentleman is Deputy Mark Barefoot. They just started today and already have been busy as...*hell,*" Deputy Matthews said while pulling up a chair to the table and gesturing for the new deputies to do the same.

Susan Davis is in her forties, petite, with long brown hair, and green eyes.

Mark Barefoot is in his thirties, tall, with his head shaved smooth, with a mustache, and brown eyes.

"I hope y'all don't mind us joining you."

"Not at all, please have a seat," Chief Adams said.

"We have had a busy day. There have been several wrecks this morning because of the dense mist we're having this morning. We also got a call from the dock manager Paul Chambers. He reported a pontoon floating to shore near the docks. There were two people on board, a man and a woman, probably the man's wife, we think. They had been fishing, and it looked like maybe they both had heart attacks and died at the same time. Which is a bit...unusual. The coroner is down at the docks now."

"They haven't been identified yet. It doesn't look like 'foul play' at the moment, but the fact that they both had a heart attack at the same time is certainly suspicious. I called the sheriff and he said to let you know, chief. You might want to send Derrick and some of the detectives to investigate further. We will be going back there *later* ourselves," Deputy Matthews said while he looked over the breakfast menu.

"We will send a team with Derrick as soon as they finish eating. Something seems to be not right about the couple dying of heart attacks at the same time. How old are they, do you think, Jim?" Chief Adams asked curiously.

"I would say they were both in their late fifties, chief. But I could be wrong."

"Derrick, I want you, Greta, and Lucinda to go to the docks and see if you can find out anything about the couple: who they are, where they are from, and where were they staying. We will have to check for next of kin also."

"Okay, chief, we will head there as soon as we leave here," Mallow replied.

"I knew it was going to be an unusual day because Derrick's bird, Speaks, talked this morning, and he said, Trouble! Trouble! Trouble!" Greta said as she took the last swallow of her coffee.

"Derrick, you named your bird, Speaks?" Deputy Matthews asked, amazed.

"Yes, I did. He only speaks when there's something ominous going on, or if Greta's coming in the apartment."

"Well, so far this week, we have had plenty of...*trouble,*" Deputy Matthews said, smiling at the waitress who was bringing his breakfast.

"Susan and Mark, how do you like your first day so far?" Lucinda asked with a slight smile.

"We didn't expect all this on the first day, but from what we heard about Lake Tisdale, the summer months can be a bit dreadful," Deputy Davis said while she took a swallow of coffee the waitress had just poured her.

"All I can say is 'welcome to Lake Tisdale' y'all," Lucinda said as she got up from the table and headed to the bathroom.

Twenty minutes later, Derrick Mallow, Greta McCall, and Lucinda Brooks were on their way to the docks in Mallow's SUV.

At the docks, it is chaos. People getting ready to go fishing and having to wait because the coroner, the sheriff, deputies, Natural Resources Department agents, and now Derrick Mallow, Greta, and Lucinda are at the docks investigating the possibility of a homicide in the deaths of the couple on the pontoon.

"Good morning, Sheriff Daniels, Coroner Potts," Mallow said as they approached the pontoon.

"Good morning, Derrick, Greta, and Lucinda. I wanted y'all here to do some checking to see if this could be a possible homicide. According to the paramedics and Coroner Potts, it looks like they mysteriously died of heart attacks," Sheriff Daniels said.

"Did they have any ID on them?" Mallow asked curiously while examining the bodies, while Greta and Lucinda inspected the pontoon.

"We didn't find any ID on them. No wallets, purses… *nothing*."

"We looked for a vehicle with a trailer without an owner at the landing, but there wasn't one. Only two vehicles with trailers were at the landing, and the people who were driving them were just getting ready to put their boats in the lake," the sheriff said, concerned.

"Mitch Johnson, an agent with the NRD, and two other agents checked the pontoon from top to bottom. They couldn't find anything. They used gloves during their inspection and were careful not to contaminate any evidence that might be on the pontoon," the sheriff said as he put his hands on his hips, leaned his head down, and exhaled heavily.

"There aren't any registration numbers on the pontoon, but there *were* numbers on it. The outline for the numbers is still on the pontoon. That's all we see," Greta said, leaning over and looking at a large gash in the metal frame of the pontoon's guardrail.

"Did the dock manager register them in his logs for a boat outing?" Lucinda asked while walking on the pontoon to the captain's chair.

In the chair was a folded piece of paper stuck under the back support. Lucinda put rubber gloves on and gently pulled the paper out. She unfolded it and discovered it was a rental agreement with Rogers Boat Rentals. It was an agreement for the weekend: Friday through Sunday. But there wasn't a name of the renters on the paper.

"Good find, Lucinda," Greta said.

"Well, we know they rented the boat, but we still don't know who they are. We will go by Rogers Boat Rentals when we leave here," Mallow said, perplexed about the mysterious deaths of the couple.

"Derrick, any ideas…at all?" the sheriff asked curiously as he watched Coroner Potts finish filling out his report.

"I am as perplexed as you are, sheriff. But we will do our best to find out what happened to this man and woman. Heart attacks at the same time don't seem logical…to me," Mallow said as he walked around the pontoon.

"Derrick, Bruce, we will need to do an autopsy on these people to see if there indeed was 'foul play' involved. The ambulance will take them back to the morgue at the sheriff's department. We can get DNA samples and see if that helps us find out who they are. But hopefully, y'all will find out something at the boat rental place," Coroner Potts said as he nodded his head, got into his car, and left.

"We will continue investigating here for a few more minutes. Then we will go to Rogers Boat Rentals to see what they can tell us. Surely, they must have used a debit or credit card to pay for the rental. But they could have paid with cash and told them not to put their names on the agreement," Mallow said as he gestured for Greta and Lucinda to follow him to the end of the dock that the boat hit before it floated to the shore.

"Derrick, we are going to head out. Another incident in the

county concerning tourists. If y'all find out anything...let me know," Sheriff Daniels said as he and the deputies left the docks.

"I will, sheriff," Mallow replied.

Mallow, Greta, and Lucinda walked to the end of the dock, and Mallow knelt and looked at the left side where the boat hit as it floated into the shore.

"Derrick, what are you looking for?" Greta asked curiously as she and Lucinda knelt beside Mallow.

"*That*! Do you two see the broken board...there," Mallow said, pointing at the support board near the guardrail.

"Yes, we do, but what does it have to do with the pontoon, Derrick?" Lucinda asked while she took a picture with her mobile phone.

"That break is new; the wood has been freshly broken. Something hit the dock hard enough to cause that. A pontoon floating with the motor not running would have scratched the board but not broken it like that."

"That was broken by another boat that probably was pulling the pontoon to shore," Mallow said as he removed his pad from his coat pocket and started writing notes.

"So there was another boat involved?" Greta asked.

"Yes, I am almost ninety-nine percent sure that another boat was involved. And if that is what happened, then this is a homicide."

"Let's check with the dock manager before we go to Rogers Boat Rentals. Maybe he can check the CCTV cameras to see if there was another boat?" Mallow said as he stood up and gestured for Greta and Lucinda to follow him.

Mallow, Greta, and Lucinda entered the dock manager's office. Paul Chambers was sitting at his desk on the computer, clicking his mouse, and hitting keys on the keyboard. The air conditioner in the window on the back wall was vibrating and making a squeaky sound.

"Come in and have a seat. I was just looking at the CCTV footage last night. I really can't see anything distinguishable because the thick mist has fogged up the camera lenses on all the cameras," Chambers said, sighing and frowning.

Mallow, Greta, and Lucinda sat down in three chairs in front of Chambers's desk. Mallow leaned over while Chambers turned the computer monitor so Mallow and the others could see the footage.

"See, Detective Mallow, nothing at all *distinguishable*."

"Yes, I can see. Hmm, we have no CCTV footage of the pontoon floating into shore or another boat that could've hit the side of the dock," Mallow said, frowning and sighing as he sat back in his chair.

"I wish we had a better picture, but that mist was terrible early this morning," Chambers said, shaking his head and watching the reactions of the three detectives.

"Well, we are wasting time here. We need to go to Rogers Boat Rentals and see what we can find out there," Mallow said as he nodded at Chambers, stood up, and said to Lucinda and Greta.

"Come on, let's go…nothing else we can do here for the moment."

Mallow, Greta, and Lucinda walked out of the dock manager's office, and Chambers exhaled quickly and frowned, walking outside his office as he watched the detectives get into the SUV and drive away.

Derrick Mallow looked in the rearview mirror as they left the docks and saw Chambers acting nervous and apprehensive.

"Chambers, I don't think he was telling us everything he knew. I believe he is holding *something*…back," Mallow said.

Up ahead of them was an old gypsy man standing on the edge of the road. His eyes were wide open, and he was talking to himself. As the SUV with the detectives got closer, Lucinda, sitting in the back seat on the right side, let down the window and could hear what the man was saying.

"It's back! Those people were *murdered* by '*the mist.*'"

"Did you two hear what that old man was saying?" Lucinda asked, pressing the button to raise the window.

"Sorry, Lucinda, we didn't hear," Greta said as she turned around to talk to Lucinda.

"It sounded like he said, 'Those people were murdered by the mist.'"

Lucinda told Greta as Mallow listened and sighed, thinking about the way Paul Chambers was acting during the time they were there and when they drove away.

"Derrick, what do you think?" Greta asked, looking at Mallow, awaiting his reply.

"I will tell you both what I think. I think this is going to be a tough case. One that I am afraid we might never be able to solve," Mallow replied reluctantly.

The detectives arrived at Rogers Boat Rentals. The location was about two miles from the Lake Tisdale Pavilion and docks, and it was located off the road about fifty yards. It was a large property, one hundred acres, and the whole property had a chain-link fence around it, with a wide entrance gate at the front.

They had fifteen center console boats and ten pontoons that they rented, and they could be purchased as well.

The owner was Nathan Rogers, white, fifty-five years old, with gray hair, blue eyes, and an average build.

The rental agent and salesman's name was Carl Anders, black, forty-one years old, with a shaved head and brown eyes.

"Well, this is the first time I have been here. I have passed it before, but never realized it was such a large place," Lucinda said, looking out the window.

Greta was on her mobile talking to the chief as Mallow drove the SUV close to the office building.

"Greta, please tell the chief that we have arrived at the boat rentals. Ask him if he can send Martin and Franklin to the local motels, hotels, and B&Bs to see if they have any guests that are missing," Mallow said as he turned the engine off and looked around the property.

"I will," Greta replied and gave Mallow the thumbs up.

Before they could get out of the car, Carl Anders was knocking on the driver's side window.

"Hello, welcome to Rogers Boat Rentals. Y'all come on and get out, and let me show you our inventory. We got just the boat you need for any outing on the lake."

Mallow smiled when he saw Lucinda frowning because the knocking on the window startled her.

Carl Anders backed away from the door and gestured for Mallow, Greta, and Lucinda to get out of the car.

Anders had been working at the boat rentals for over five years. He was the only rental agent with the boat rental company.

"Hello, I am Detective Derrick Mallow, and this is Detective Greta McCall and Detective Lucinda Brooks. We are here investigating an accident and possible homicide that happened out on the lake sometime in the early morning. We found a rental agreement in the pontoon that the couple was found dead on. So, we are here to see what you can tell us about the renters. They didn't have any IDs on them, and the boat registration numbers and tag had been removed from the boat."

Carl Anders was speechless. He looked all around, scratching his head, and pacing around.

"My God…detective, I am at a loss for words. I didn't expect something like this…today."

"My name is Carl Anders. I am the rental agent here at Rogers Boat Rentals. I will try to help…all I can, detectives."

"Why weren't the renters' names on the agreement? Did

anyone here at the boat rentals remove the boat ID, and the registration numbers and tag? Did you write down the information on their vehicle?" Greta asked, holding a pad under her arm.

Meanwhile, Lucinda was walking around some of the other boats looking for missing IDs and registrations.

"All these boats have the IDs, registrations, and tags on them," Lucinda told Mallow and Greta.

"We didn't remove any IDs or registrations from the boat. The renters didn't want their names on the rental agreement. They paid cash and said that they didn't want anyone to know that they were here in Lake Tisdale. Yes, ma'am, I did write down the information on their vehicle. It was a rental also. It was a late model four-door sedan, blue, with a white top. The license plate was a dealer's tag. They rented the car from a used car place in Summings. The name of the used car place was called 'Randy's Used Cars.' The name was on the license plate frame," Anders said, holding his palm over his forehead with his feet moving from side to side.

"Calm down, Mr. Anders, we are here just to ask questions. We are not saying that you or your company are responsible for the deaths of the couple," Mallow said, trying to reassure the rental agent.

"Did they use their vehicle to take the boat and trailer to the lake, or did y'all take the boat there for them?" Mallow asked.

"Yes, they hooked the boat and trailer to their vehicle. The trailer had a license plate on it, and the frame had Rogers Boat Rentals on it. It was a silver trailer with a black bumper and tongue," Anders replied, exhaling nervously.

"I probably need to call the owner, Nathan Rogers, and tell him what has happened. He didn't have a long conversation with those folks. He just said hello when they walked through the office to my desk," Anders said, scratching his head.

"Mr. Anders, you have told us what we need to know. Don't bother the owner. If there is anything else we need to ask you, we can call. Can I have your mobile number...please?" Greta said while writing down notes on a pad.

"Yes, ma'am, my mobile number is 843-777-0052."

"Derrick, Lucinda, you two have anything else you want to ask Mr. Anders?"

"I think we found out what we needed here. We will need to see what Martin and Franklin found out at the hotels and B&Bs," Mallow replied, looking around the lot.

"We will go and grab a bite, and then after we check with Martin and Franklin, we will check out the used car place in Summings," Mallow said.

"Thanks, Mr. Anders, you have been a great help," Mallow said with a slight smile as the three detectives got into the SUV and left the boat rentals.

CHAPTER 2

Mallow, Greta, and Lucinda stop at Jimbo's Bar and Grill in the middle of town. It is fast approaching lunchtime, and the detective trio is getting hungry.

They get out of the car, and Mallow sniffs and smells the Double Cheeseburger Specials cooking on the grill.

"You two smell that enticing aroma coming from inside?" Mallow asked as he walked up to the door and held it open for Greta and Lucinda.

"It does smell good in here. Either that, or I am extremely hungry," Lucinda said, shaking her head as she watched some of the customers enjoying their lunches.

They quickly find themselves a table and start eagerly looking for Ruth. Ruth is the waitress along with Misty today.

Mallow holds his hand up when he sees Ruth at one of the back tables. Ruth sees him, smiles, and points one finger up, to let Mallow know she is on the way shortly.

"Hello, Derrick, Greta, and Lucinda. What will it be today, guys?" Ruth asked after putting three glasses of ice water on the table.

Lucinda looked at Mallow and Greta, smiled, and said confidently, "We will have three Double Cheeseburger Specials and three large colas, darling."

"Very good, I will get the cooks right on these orders, and they should be ready shortly. Anything I can get y'all in the meantime?" Ruth asked while giving a nod to another customer at the table next to the detectives.

"Derrick, I know you love the special, but doesn't it give you heartburn?" Greta asked, looking at the other customers in the bar and grill.

"Yes, it does. That is why I carry these antacid pills with me."

"The special doesn't bother me. It just makes me gain a few…pounds," Lucinda said reluctantly with a slight smile.

"It's real busy here today. Summertime, I guess, everybody trying to get a fast lunch before going fishing, swimming, skiing, boating, or whatever," Greta said as she took a swallow of water from her glass.

"Yes, it is busy today. A lot of strange-looking people in here. Hope they all are here to have fun and enjoy themselves, and not get into mischief," Lucinda said as she watched two men at one of the back tables watching the detectives closely.

"Derrick, you look like you are in…deep thought, sitting there," Greta said, intrigued.

"Sorry, I didn't mean to ignore you two. I was thinking about that couple that was found this morning. A lot of things aren't adding up. Why didn't they give their names to the boat renters, and why did someone take the IDs and registration tags off the pontoon? Hmm, it is a big mystery, but why is it a mystery?" Mallow said, still in deep thought.

"Well, we will talk about it later. Our specials have arrived. Yum! Yum!" Lucinda said, smiling and inhaling the deliciously smelling double cheeseburger and Jumbo fries.

"I agree with Lucinda, let's eat," Greta said, smiling and taking a couple of fries from her plate.

Just as the detectives were starting to enjoy their specials, the two men who were watching them started walking toward the exit. One of the men pauses and looks at Lucinda and Greta, gives a snarl, and then proceeds to the exit.

"Wonder what's wrong with him?" Lucinda asked while taking a bite of her cheeseburger.

"Who knows," Mallow said, disturbed about the way the man acted.

"Well, they are gone now. Let's enjoy our lunch while we can," Greta said.

Ten minutes later, Ruth came back to the detectives' table and checked with them to see if they needed anything else. "Is everything okay, guys? Can I get y'all something else? More cola, dessert…another cheeseburger?" Ruth asked with a smile as she watched Mallow finish the last bite of his burger.

"We are good, Ruth. Can you bring our check, please?" Mallow asked with a smile.

"Sure, will it be three checks or just one?"

"Just one, Ruth, I am treating the ladies today," Mallow said, smiling at Greta and Lucinda.

"Thanks, Derrick, that is so kind of you," Lucinda said.

"You are such a good friend, Derrick," Greta said, smiling at him and Lucinda.

"Thanks, ladies. I need one of you to go to 'Maps' on your phone, and type in Randy's Used Cars. I am not exactly sure where it is located in Summings. I think it might be off Highway 378."

"I will do it, Derrick," Greta said, opening the Maps app on her phone.

Ruth was bringing them their check for their lunch, and she saw Greta typing in the name of the used car sales.

"I didn't mean to look. I just saw you typing in Randy's Used Cars. That business is located just off the interstate on 378. After you get off the interstate, take a right, and the used car sales are on the left. You can't miss it. There is a huge sign out front."

"Thanks, Ruth," Greta said politely.

Ruth handed Mallow the check, and Mallow wrote in the tip

amount on the check and gave her his debit card. She walked behind the bar to process the card. A few minutes later, she brought it back to Mallow and said, "Thanks for the tip, Derrick."

Mallow was very generous; he gave her a twenty-dollar tip.

"Thank you for the good service, Ruth," Mallow, Greta, and Lucinda said simultaneously.

"Y'all welcome, come back soon."

The three detectives, now full of the specials, proceeded out the door and into the SUV to begin the journey to Randy's Used Cars.

"Greta, call Martin and see if he and Franklin found out anything at the hotels, motels, and B&Bs," Mallow said while thinking, *this is not making any sense…at all.*

Greta called Franklin on his mobile after not being able to reach him on the police two-way radios.

"Franklin, hey, did you and Martin find out anything?"

"No, Greta, we didn't. Nobody had reported missing guests at their establishments. All their out-of-state guests were registered and accounted for," Franklin said, popping a bubble with his gum.

"What's wrong with your two-way police radio, Franklin?" Greta asked curiously.

"Nothing, as I know of. It was working earlier when I talked to the chief," Franklin responded.

"I tried several times to get you on it. Is Martin's working? I tried his radio, too," Greta asked.

"Damn, sorry, Greta. I forgot to turn mine on," Martin said reluctantly.

"Franklin, can you and Martin do one other thing for us?" Greta asked.

"Sure, what do you want us to do?"

"Go to the docks and the landings, and see if there is a vehicle and boat trailer that is parked with a Rogers Boat Rental License on the trailer. The sheriff and the deputies have already checked and said there wasn't a vehicle and trailer left stranded. We need to double-check that," Greta said while writing notes on her pad and gesturing for Mallow to make the left turn into Randy's Used Cars.

"We will do it. We will let you guys know what we find out," Franklin said.

Mallow pulled into the driveway and parked the car in front of the office. The office building is a double-wide mobile home.

Randy's Used Cars is owned by Randy Olsen. He is fifty-one years old, bald, white, green-eyed, average build, and is a heavy smoker.

There is only one salesman, other than Olsen. His name is Johnny McBrien; he is forty-two years old, white, green-eyed, tall, and wears blue-jean coveralls and a white tee-shirt most of the time.

The business is located on a two-acre lot. It has a wooden fence all around it, with a wooden gate. On the lot, there are about twenty vehicles, cars, and trucks for sale, and there are five vehicles for rental only.

The three detectives get out of the SUV and walk up the steps to the office door. Mallow turns the knob on the door, but the door is locked. He walks over to a window and looks in while Greta and Lucinda are looking around the lot to see if they see anyone. Mallow knocks at the door, but no one comes to open it.

"Derrick, we don't see anyone walking around the car lot. There aren't any other cars parked that might have customers walking around looking at the inventory," Greta said.

"They must be closed, Derrick," Lucinda said as she walked down the steps and cautiously walked around the mobile home to the backside.

"No other cars parked here either, and I checked the back entrance. It is locked as well," Greta said.

"Hmm, okay, I guess we made a trip for *nothing,*" Mallow said, sighing and shaking his head.

"Well, you would think they would have closed the wooden gate and locked it...wouldn't you?" Greta asked while she watched a car slow down and then speed up when they passed the used car lot.

"Wonder who they are?" Lucinda asked Greta.

"I don't know," Greta replied, perplexed.

"What next, Derrick?" Lucinda asked as they walked to the SUV, opened the doors, and sat down.

"We need to call the chief. Check with the sheriff's department, the coroner, and the deputies to see if they found out anything about the identities of the man and woman."

"Greta, please, write down the phone number here on your pad," Mallow asked politely.

Mallow took one last look around the used car lot and noticed an old model sedan in the far corner of the parking lot. It looked like the back end was up against the fence.

"What's wrong, Derrick?" Greta asked as Lucinda looked at Mallow, wondering what he was looking at.

"That old sedan parked over there looks out of place, and it's up against the fence," Mallow said while in deep thought.

He started the SUV and drove over to where the old sedan was parked. Mallow studied the car carefully but didn't get out of the SUV to check the inside.

"What, Derrick?" Greta and Lucinda said at the same time.

"I'm sorry, that *car,* there's something about it that's... *not right.*"

"But I don't know what it is. It may be just me, or..." Mallow said suspiciously as he turned the SUV around and they headed for the exit.

After they left Randy's Used Cars, Mallow called the chief on his mobile. Greta and Lucinda were looking over their notes. The two women agreed that something at the used car lot wasn't right. It wasn't a holiday, and the posted hours on the office door did not agree with the business being closed today.

"Hello, chief, I was calling to check the status of the identities of the couple. Has the coroner been able to find out anything with the DNA analysis?" Mallow asked while still thinking about the old sedan parked against the fence at the used car lot.

"Hello, Derrick. There is still nothing to report. We don't have anything that can help us find the identities of those two people," the chief replied.

"We haven't found anything either, chief. We were hoping that we would find some good leads at Randy's Used Cars. But, they were closed for some unknown reason," Mallow informed the chief as Lucinda tapped on the window, pointing at the old gypsy man standing on the side of the road.

"Y'all, look, that old gypsy man is standing there with his hands up and appears to be shouting something," Lucinda said, shaking her head because, until today, no one had seen the man for a long time.

Mallow and Greta looked and then looked at Lucinda. She was still shaking her head.

"That old man has always... freaked me out. He ain't normal, always shouting out crazy... shit," Lucinda said apprehensively.

Mallow ended his call with the chief and informed Greta and Lucinda of what the chief told him.

"They haven't found anything out... yet. So, the chief wants us to come by the department for a briefing. He is checking with Franklin and Martin to see if they are having any luck at the docks and landings," Mallow said, disappointed.

It was late on Friday evening, and Franklin and Martin had been busy searching the landings and docks and asking questions. But they hadn't been able to find out anything about the whereabouts of the car and the boat trailer.

"Franklin, you copy me?" the chief asked over the police two-way radio.

"Yes, chief, I copy you," Franklin replied.

"Did you guys find out anything?"

"No, sir, we looked everywhere. We checked the docks' parking lots and the boat landings… but we didn't have any luck," Franklin said while looking at Martin, who was exhausted from their long search.

"Well, call it a day there. And come back to the department. We are going to have a meeting as soon as everyone is here. We have to decide how we are going to go forward in this investigation. The sheriff told me that there is a possibility that the 'Feds' might get involved," the chief said, sniffling, sighing, and then smiling when Gail brought him a coffee and a doughnut.

"Okay, chief, we are going to wrap things up here and head to the department. We will see y'all… soon."

The chief and Franklin ended their radio conversation, and Franklin and Martin left the docks and landings.

It was getting misty again around the lake area, and it was becoming thick. This was an unusual occurrence because the mist appeared over the lake and town in the mornings.

As Franklin and Martin drove away from the lake, they saw the old gypsy man standing on the side of the road with his head up and his arms raised high, chanting.

CHAPTER 3

Chief Adams was in the new briefing room at the Lake Tisdale Police Department. He had laid a folder on the table with today's briefing notes.

He sat down, held his head, and folded his hands together on top of the folder.

In walked Assistant Chief Mason Briggs. He looked behind him and gestured for Gail Stephens to join him and the chief.

Mallow and the others were still en route and would arrive shortly.

"Gail, can I please get up to pour coffees for everyone and set them around the table?" the chief asked politely while looking at Mason Briggs and shaking his head.

"Mason, I was hoping we would have an easy… weekend. Alice and I were going to go fishing on the lake on Saturday. Looks like that might be out now."

"Chief, things will probably work out, so you and Alice can 'wet a hook,' sir," the assistant chief said optimistically.

"Maybe it will. Ah! Thank you, Gail, I do appreciate you doing this," the chief said as he picked up his cup of coffee and sniffed the aroma for a few moments before taking a swallow.

"Thanks, Gail," the assistant chief said as she handed him his cup of coffee.

Gail Stephens smiled and sat down across from the assistant chief with her coffee in hand and said, "Y'all are welcome. You know when the others are going to arrive, chief?"

"Hopefully, they will be here in a few more minutes."

The new briefing room was located at the back end of the police department. It had a large conference table with video, audio, internet, and speakerphone capabilities. There were twelve brown leather chairs with silver frames around the table —six to each side.

The walls were painted green, and the floor was square tiled with green and white stripes on each tile.

On the walls were photos of retired and deceased police officers. Greg Hustess's photo was the largest of the photos. There were photos of present-day police officers and the new detectives of the "Homicide Investigations Department."

There was even a photo of Mallow's bird, Speaks, a Red-Headed Finch.

"You know what would make this coffee taste… better? Some glazed doughnuts," Gail said with a smile.

"Too bad, Lucinda and Franklin finished them up… earlier today," the assistant chief said, disappointed, with a slight chuckle.

Suddenly, there was laughing and giggling heard in the hallway. It was Greta and Lucinda laughing about a joke she told Greta and Mallow. Mallow wasn't laughing; he was just shaking his head and grinning.

"Well, y'all did make it, after all," Gail Stephens said, smiling brightly because when Mallow walked into the briefing room behind Greta and Lucinda, he was carrying two boxes of fresh glazed doughnuts from Toby's Bakery and Coffee Shop.

Following behind him were Martin and Franklin, both smiling from ear to ear.

"Come on in and have a seat, and thanks for bringing the

doughnuts, guys," the chief said, smiling and picking up two doughnuts from one of the boxes.

"We are all here except for Mayor Brooks. He said to start without him. That he would be here shortly," the chief said, opening the folder before him.

"Okay, we all got coffee and doughnuts, so let's get this briefing started… shall we?" the chief said as he took another bite out of the doughnut and pulled out a couple of papers from the folder.

"Yeah, I want to thank y'all for the doughnuts," Franklin smiled, delighted to have fresh glazed doughnuts.

Martin and Mason Briggs just nodded their heads because their mouths were full of doughnuts.

"Our top case is, of course, the mysterious deaths by heart attack of the couple found at the docks this morning in the pontoon. We have all been busy investigating, and so far… we haven't any leads… whatsoever. We will not know anything about the DNA results until tomorrow… now, because the Feds are getting involved with this case as well. They are talking to Sheriff Daniels and The State Law Enforcement Police. We may have to work with the Feds and the state police along with the sheriff's department," the chief said.

"I would like a report on the investigation that you have done… so far. It's getting late, and I know you are all enervated. I know I am. So, we won't go around the table with that information."

"Hmm, I just got a text from the mayor. He isn't going to be able to make it. Well, in a way… I guess that is a good thing. Okay, I am afraid that we are going to have to work full shifts tomorrow. I know that some of you had plans, but I am afraid we are going to have to postpone them for now," the chief said reluctantly and frowning.

"If no one has anything they want to add to the briefing. Let's call it a day and go home and get some rest. I will see you all here in the morning at seven o'clock."

Everyone was ready to call it a day and was glad the chief was *too*. So, they all said their goodbyes and headed for home.

Mallow and Greta got into the SUV, exhaled, and started on their way home. They were going to make a quick stop at Jimbo's Bar and Grill to pick up two Cheeseburger Specials.

Mallow and Greta made a quick stop at Jimbo's to pick up two Cheeseburger Specials. Greta was thinking ahead, and before they arrived at the police department to attend the briefing, she ordered their Cheeseburger Specials to go. So they were ready for pick up as soon as they arrived.

It was getting late, and the wind began to blow briskly. Before they got to Jimbo's, Greta saw the old gypsy man standing on the side of the road chanting something with his arms raised high.

"Derrick, there is the gypsy man… again. Do you think he is just crazy, or does he actually know something?" Greta asked as she lowered the passenger side window to see if she could hear what he said.

As they passed by the old man, Greta couldn't make out what he was saying. So, she let the window up and shook her head.

"Greta, we will talk with him... soon. But not tonight. Let's pick up our dinner, go home, enjoy it, and rest," Mallow said, still thinking about the old sedan at Randy's Used Cars.

A few minutes later, Mallow drove into Jimbo's parking lot. He parked the SUV near the door, and Greta got out and went inside to pay for the pick-up order. It didn't take her more than a few minutes, and she came out smiling, inhaling the delicious aroma from the bag that contained the Cheeseburger Specials.

"My treat *tonight*, Derrick. Tomorrow it will be your turn," Greta said, smiling as Mallow started the SUV and they began their journey home.

Mallow looked at Greta, smiled, and nodded his head.

They didn't see the old gypsy man on their way to the apartment. The old man concerned Greta.

She had a feeling the old man knew something, and Mallow was still perplexed about the old sedan at Randy's Used Cars.

"Derrick, why do you think the Feds are getting involved in this case? Do you think it is because of the mysterious way the couple died?" Greta asked while sneaking a couple of fries from the bag.

Mallow sighed, thought for a second, and said, "It could be that, or it could be that the couple was under 'witness protection.'"

"You may be right. I didn't think about that," Greta said while eating one of the fries from the bag she was holding.

Mallow exhaled and said, "We are home," as they pulled into the parking space for their apartment.

When they entered the apartment, Speaks was flying around the living room in a circle, saying, "'Old sedan, Randy's,' 'old gypsy man.'" He was repeating it over and over. Then Speaks flew into his cage, looked at Mallow, and said, "No food, and no water."

Greta looked at Mallow and he looked at her, and they both said simultaneously, "I thought you fed the *bird... this morning.*"

"Will you get the food ready, Greta? I will feed Speaks."

"I will do it, Derrick," Greta said, alarmed at what the bird was saying when they entered the apartment.

After they got Speaks settled down with his birdseed and water dinner, Mallow and Greta sat at the kitchen table and enjoyed their Cheeseburger Specials.

"I have to admit, Derrick, Jimbo's cheeseburgers are the best I have ever had," Greta said while taking another bite.

"Yes, I would have to agree with you... one hundred percent, Greta."

Then they heard Speaks again. He was in his cage, chirping loudly, then the bird repeated, "'Old Sedan, Randy's,' 'old gypsy man.'"

"Wonder what's up with Speaks, Derrick?" Greta said as she wiped her mouth and started walking toward the living room.

She turned around and said to Mallow with a grin, "I cooked, you have to clean up and wash the dishes."

"What's wrong, Speaks? Are you trying to tell us something?" Greta asked while reaching inside the cage and patting the bird on the head.

Mallow finished cleaning up and joined Greta in the living room, where she was watching a game show on the TV.

"Do you think we should go and check the old sedan at the used car lot? And maybe try to talk to the old gypsy... tomorrow?" Greta asked as she sat down in her recliner beside Mallow's.

"We will tell the chief, and after our meeting in the morning, we will see if he wants us to proceed with it," Mallow replied while leaning back in the recliner.

After watching an hour or so of TV, Greta and Mallow walked to the bedroom and went to bed. Speaks flew out of his cage and followed them. He usually sleeps on top of the headboard at night.

CHAPTER 4

It's six o'clock on Saturday morning, and the clock radio alarm blares on the nightstand on Mallow's side of the bed. Speaks is on top of it, chirping away, and the bird starts to speak, "Get up, Derrick. Get up, Greta."

Mallow reaches out with his hand and hits the "Alarm Silence Button" on the clock radio.

He taps Greta on the shoulder and softly says, "Greta, darling, it's time to 'rise and shine.'"

Greta wiggles her nose, exhales, and replies, "Give me another five minutes... *please*."

"Greta, it is after six, darling. Get up, we have just enough time to shower, feed Speaks, and head on to work. We can get breakfast at Toby's after the meeting this morning. Now, *please* get up."

"Okay, I got the shower first," Greta said as she slowly got up and wobbled to the bathroom.

"I will feed Speaks. And I will brew some coffee. Hurry up, I need to shower, *too*," Mallow said, yawning as he slipped on his shoes and walked to the kitchen.

Forty minutes later, they were in the SUV and headed for the police department. Both yawning and looking almost like "zombies."

Yesterday was a stressful day, and the morning came... too quickly.

"Did you feed Speaks, Derrick?" Greta asked, yawning and taking a swallow of coffee from her insulated coffee mug.

"Yes, I did. And he was eating his birdseed when we left the apartment."

As they were entering the town and almost at the police station, they saw the old gypsy man on the sidewalk. This early morning, he wasn't chanting; he was just watching Mallow and Greta as they passed by in the SUV.

"There's our friend again, Greta," Mallow said, pointing at the old man.

"Well, he's an 'early bird,' isn't he," Greta replied with a yawn and took another sip of coffee.

Mallow turned into the driveway to the parking lot and had to slam on the brakes because Lucinda was strolling toward the back entrance, texting on her phone.

Lucinda was startled and looked at Mallow and Greta nervously.

Mallow lowered the driver-side window and asked, "Lucinda, you *okay*?"

She was gasping, panting, and breathing heavily. Then she closed her eyes and replied, "Yeah, I'm okay, Derrick. I didn't see you all coming up."

Greta was holding her chest because she knew they were going to hit Lucinda.

"Derrick, that *scared* the... *shit* out of... me," Greta said, still shocked by what happened.

Mallow parked the SUV, and they walked over to where Lucinda was now sitting on the steps with her palm over her forehead and crying.

"Lucinda, I am so... sorry. I didn't mean..." Mallow apologized.

"It's okay, Derrick. I was on the phone with my sister in North Carolina. Our mother had a heart attack, and they had to rush her to the hospital by ambulance. I have got to tell the chief I need to go and check on her and my sister."

"I am sorry to hear that, Lucinda. If there is anything Greta and I can do...?"

"Thanks, Derrick and Greta," Lucinda said as Mallow and Greta helped her up the steps and into the hallway.

Lucinda is distraught, and she is still crying. Gail Stephens makes Lucinda a cup of coffee and hands it to her.

The chief is in his office on the phone with Sheriff Daniels and doesn't know yet about Lucinda's mother.

Lucinda sits down near Gail and Greta at the receptionist's desk. She is feeling despondent, wiping away tears with a tissue that Gail handed her.

Franklin and Martin are pouring themselves a coffee and grabbing a couple of doughnuts.

Mallow pours himself a coffee, picks up a doughnut, and sits down near the women while Franklin and Martin lean against the wall.

"Wonder what the chief and the sheriff are discussing?" Martin asked curiously.

"They are probably talking about the Feds coming to town and getting involved in this... mysterious death or murder case," Franklin replied while looking at Lucinda, and then holding his head down.

A few moments later, the chief finishes talking with the sheriff and walks into the hallway. He looks around, sighs, and says, "This is a gloomy bunch... this morning."

"Chief, Lucinda's mother had a heart attack. She is in the hospital in North Carolina," Mallow informs the chief.

"Oh my God, Lucinda, you all right?" the chief asked, concerned.

"I am... okay, chief. I gotta go to North Carolina to be with her," Lucinda said, trying to hold back tears.

"Sure, Lucinda, take all the time you need, but I don't want you to go... alone. You are distraught, and your mind is on your mother. Gail, can you go with Lucinda to North Carolina?" the chief asked sympathetically while putting his hand on Lucinda's shoulder.

"Of course, chief. I will go with her, and I will drive, Lucinda. You can call and check with your sister while we drive. I am ready... when you are, Lucinda," Gail said while pouring herself and Lucinda another cup of coffee.

"Okay, Lucinda, if we can do anything to help... please, let us know," the chief said as he looked around at the other officers who were feeling heartbroken for Lucinda.

"Lucinda, y'all drive safe, and please, keep us informed, dear," Greta said, wiping the tears from her eyes.

The chief sighed and said, "I talked with the sheriff, and he said that the Feds would be here sometime today. We will be asked to inform them about anything we know about this case... so far. I want Franklin and Martin to return to the landings and docks and investigate further. We have got to find out what happened to the vehicle and the boat trailer."

"Derrick and Greta, I need you two to go back to the boat rentals and the used car lot. Maybe Randy's will be open... today. Check with the owner at the boat rentals," the chief said while slowly taking a sip of coffee.

"We will do it, chief," Mallow said, pouring himself and Greta another cup of coffee.

"We're on it, chief," Martin said, nodding his head.

"Lucinda, Gail, you two need to get on the road. Take one of the cruisers, just in case you have to get there faster," the chief insisted as he picked up a doughnut and turned toward the front door when the receptionist's phone rang.

Gail picked up the receiver, put the call on speaker, and said, "Lake Tisdale Police Department, how may I help you?"

On the other end of the phone was the old gypsy man. His voice was hoarse, and he sounded terrified.

"I need to talk with Mallow and the lady detective about the couple that died at the docks. I am at my home. You folks know where I live. Tell them to hurry, *please*."

Then he hung up quickly.

"Well, wonder what Calvin wants to tell us?" the chief said as he and the others looked stunned by what the old gypsy man said.

"Derrick, you and Greta, go to his house and talk with him. I don't know what he's going to tell you two, but it might be helpful. He talks crazy most of the time. Who knows, he might be right about what he is saying," the chief said reluctantly as he and the others waved goodbye to Lucinda and Gail as they left the department.

"Y'all, *please* be careful, and Lucinda, we all wish a speedy recovery for your mother... dear," Greta said as she and Mallow followed them out of the department to get on their way to the old man's house.

Calvin Miller is the old gypsy man, even though he doesn't have a gypsy name. He is seventy-one years old, of average build, with gray hair and green eyes. He usually wears faded blue jeans and a straw hat. He lives by himself in an old camper about a mile down the road from Rogers Boat Rental.

After everyone left but the chief and the assistant chief, the chief looked at Mason Briggs and said, "It's gonna be another tough... day, Mason."

"Mason, it looks like you are going to be the receptionist today, and I am gonna be the 'street patrol.'"

"Hopefully, the mayor and the town council will decide on the other officers we are going to get," Mason said as he looked out the window at the front door.

"Chief, I think we need to take a breakfast break. Let's go to Toby's...I'm buying."

"You talked me into it, Mason."

They both started to open the door at the same time, and then the chief said politely, "After you, Mason."

"No chief, *after*...you," Mason said, opening the door and gesturing for the chief to go first.

Mallow and Greta arrived at the home of the old gypsy man, also known by his name, Calvin Miller. The camper was beaten up, and the roof was rusty and looked like it was coming apart on the ends.

"Whew," Greta said as she opened the SUV door.

The grass was knee-high, and there was trash all over the property.

On the tongue end of the camper, there was an old blue and white bicycle with both tires flat, and from under the trailer, a red-tabby cat came out meowing and purring.

Mallow got out and rubbed his nose because there was a repugnant odor all around the camper. The wind was blowing briskly, making the stench that much more extreme.

"Have you ever smelt such a stench, Derrick?" Greta asked, holding her nose as they both walked to the door of the camper.

"No, I haven't."

Mallow knocked on the door and stepped back. Inside, they could hear metal clanking together. Then there were footsteps walking toward the door.

The old gypsy man opened the door and said, "You two the detectives?"

"Yes, sir, we are the detectives," Mallow replied.

"Well, don't just stand there, come on in," the old man invited, stepping away from the door and taking a seat in a recliner next to the back wall.

Inside the camper, it was dirty, and clothes were lying around everywhere. The sink was full of dishes, pots, and pans.

"Y'all can have a seat on the sofa. It's clean…ain't no dirt on it."

"Your name is Calvin Miller. Is that right, sir?" Greta asked as she slowly sat down on the sofa, followed by Mallow.

"Yes, ma'am, that is my name," the old man replied while spitting into an old metal pot on a table by the recliner.

"Why do the townspeople call you 'the old gypsy man,' sir?" Mallow asked curiously, looking around at all the mess and junk that was spread around the camper.

"That's because my momma was a gypsy, and my daddy was part Indian."

"Okay," Mallow said while pulling out his notepad and pen from his coat pocket.

"What do you want to tell us, Mr. Miller?" Mallow asked, then startled because a cat came out from behind the sofa and rubbed against his pants leg.

"Don't mind the cat. He is just curious…he won't hurt ya," the old man said with a frown, and then he spit in the pot again.

Greta pulled out her notepad and pen and started taking notes with Mallow after the old man started talking.

"What I want to tell you two is, a long time ago this town didn't exist. There was only the lake. There were a lot of people here who didn't live in houses. They lived in tents along the banks of the lake. In the late spring and early summer, the morning mist would be so thick you could touch it, and it would feel like touching a white sheet floating above the ground. One day, a young couple was wading in the water by the bank and holding hands when a loud noise was heard behind them. They were startled, of course, and got out of the water and started running back to their tent. Suddenly, the mist became dense, and they couldn't see where they were going. They got separated and somehow drifted far apart. Then the loud noise happened again, and they mysteriously disappeared. The couple had vanished. They were never seen again. Most of the elders of that time say that they were 'murdered by the mist.' I know it sounds kinda crazy, but honestly, that was the way they told the story."

"And to this day, there have been mysterious occurrences every five years at the lake when the mist comes. I don't know why it's when the mist is the most dense...but that seems to be the cycle."

"The reason it stinks so bad outside is that I have put out herbs and mixtures of certain leaves from the trees to keep the mist away from my camper."

The old man inhaled deeply after telling Mallow and Greta the story, and tears flowed down his cheeks.

Mallow and Greta were surprised by the story the old man told. They started writing down everything the man said, but for some reason, their hands became stiff and they couldn't write anymore.

"You two probably think that the story I just told you is a lie. But I assure you it is not, because the young couple that disappeared were my mother and father," the old gypsy man said, wiping tears from his eyes.

"My grandfather and my grandmother, along with the local law enforcement in the adjacent county, looked for my mother and father for years. But never found a single trace of them. I was only one year old at the time they disappeared. My grandfather and grandmother took me in and raised me," the old man said while looking down at the floor, and then he sighed.

The story dumbfounded Mallow and Greta. Also, they didn't know why their hands got stiff at the same time while they were writing.

Derrick Mallow always carried his small tape recorder in his pocket and he did turn it on when he got out of the SUV. So, he knew they had everything the old man said on tape. At least that's what he thought.

"Mr. Miller, is there anything else, sir?" Mallow asked,

putting away his notepad and pen. His hands were still a bit stiff but slowly returning to normal.

"I have told you two a lot more than I have told anyone in this town. I trust you two," the old man said as he looked at Mallow and Greta and then out of the back window.

"So, Mr. Miller, you think that the couple that died from heart attacks were murdered by the mist?" Greta asked while wiping her runny nose and sniffling.

"Sorry, my allergies are acting up…again," Greta said.

"I do believe that."

"That is why I said it. I don't know why it happens. I don't to this day know why the mist took my mother and father. I just know that the mist is evil," the old man said, standing up and holding his head down.

"Mr. Miller, I want to thank you for talking to us. If you can think of anything else related to the case, please let us know," Mallow said as he and Greta handed the old man one of their cards with their contact information.

The old man wiped his eyes again and nodded as Mallow and Greta opened the door and started walking toward the SUV. Mallow took another look around the property, shook his head, and then looked at Greta who was opening the passenger's side door.

"What, Derrick?" Greta asked curiously.

Mallow opened the door to the driver's side, put his hands on the top of the SUV, and said, "What happened to us in there? Why did our hands go stiff?"

"I don't know, maybe it was something inside the camper or the herbs and leaves around this property. We might be allergic," Greta said as she sat down in the seat waiting on Mallow.

Mallow started the SUV and they left the old man's property and headed for Randy's Used Cars.

CHAPTER 5

Martin and Franklin arrive at one of the boat landings. There are two boaters standing by a boat on a trailer. They are talking and smoking cigarettes. They see the police cruiser approaching and quickly put out the cigarettes. They get in the car and expeditiously leave the landing. Before they can get on the road, Martin gets out of the cruiser, rushes to their car, and flags them down.

"Hello, gentlemen. Don't be alarmed; I just wanted to ask you guys something. We are looking for a boat trailer and car that is missing. The boat trailer belonged to Rogers Boat Rentals, and the car was from Randy's Used Cars. The trailer was silver and black and had a Rogers Boat Rentals plate on it. The car was an older four-door sedan, blue with a white top…I believe. It had dealer tags on it from Randy's Used Cars," Martin said while watching the reaction of the two young men.

The two young boaters were probably in their late twenties. They were dressed in fisherman's clothes, including the white fisherman's hats with the hooks and lures attached to them.

The driver of the car looked at Martin and Franklin carefully. Franklin was standing at the back of the car, looking at the license plate and the boat and trailer. The trailer was silver and black, but there was no license plate frame with Rogers Boat Rentals. The car they were driving was an older four-door sedan, red with white stripes.

"Officer, we ain't seen a boat trailer like the one you... described. We've been here since this morning, and we were the only ones on this landing," the driver said as he lit another cigarette.

"Okay, thank you, gentlemen. Have a great rest of your day," Martin said with a slight smile.

After the two boaters drove away, Martin and Franklin looked around the landing, and walked into the nearby woods but didn't find anything.

"Well, this was the only boat landing we hadn't searched, Martin. Where do we go...next?" Franklin asked while pulling out a stick of gum from his shirt pocket.

"I say we go to the pavilion and ask around to see if anyone may have seen the trailer or the car and trailer," Martin said as he got into the passenger side of the cruiser and buckled up, waiting for Franklin to get in the cruiser.

"Are we on a 'wild goose chase,' Martin?" Franklin asked.

"I am not a detective like you, Lucinda, Derrick, and Greta. I am just a police officer," Franklin said, agitated because he didn't get promoted to detective.

"Franklin, even though we are detectives, we are police officers. And to tell you the truth...I have heard rumors that they were going to make you a detective with the rest of us...soon."

"So, stop bellyaching, and let's see what we can find at the pavilion. Okay?" Martin said, looking out the window and shaking his head.

Franklin got into the cruiser, buckled up, and started the engine. They left the boat landing on their way to the pavilion.

"I'm sorry, Martin, for being such an...asshole," Franklin apologized while looking out the window and putting another piece of gum in his mouth.

"I don't...know, sometimes I feel like an outsider in this

department. I have felt so alone after my wife…died," Franklin said sadly.

"You are not an outsider. You are an important part of the police department. And whether you know it or not…you have a lot of friends there and in Lake Tisdale that care about you…a lot," Martin replied.

"Okay, here we are at the pavilion. You okay, Franklin?" Martin asked, concerned.

They arrived at the pavilion. There were a lot of cars in the parking lot. Several people were at the entrance on the outside smoking cigarettes because cigarette smoking is not allowed inside the pavilion.

Martin and Franklin got out of the police cruiser and headed for the entrance. They stopped and chatted with some of the people outside.

The wind was beginning to blow briskly, and the clouds were changing from white to gray. There was a storm brewing, and storms here at the lake in the summertime can be very profound.

"Hello, I am Officer Martin, and this is my partner, Officer Stokes. We are here looking for a car and trailer that was abandoned. Have y'all seen a car and trailer that has been parked for a long while? It pertains to the couple who were found dead on a pontoon at the docks," Martin asked while looking at the reactions of the people standing outside.

"I haven't seen a car and trailer," a young man replied as he put out his cigarette in the outside cigarette disposal can.

"Does that go for the rest of you?" Franklin asked curiously while popping a bubble with his gum.

The rest of the people nodded their heads, and Martin sighed. Franklin blew another bubble, and they entered the pavilion.

The inside of the pavilion was crowded. There was elbow room only. Inside, people were playing video games, the pool tables, the basketball toss game, and the miniature bowling alley.

At the concessions, people were sitting and eating fast food and drinks.

"Is the manager here today?" Martin asked the cook at the concessions grill.

"No, sir, he's not here today. He will be back tomorrow."

"Okay, maybe you can answer a question for *me*...if you will?" Martin asked.

"I will try, sir, if I can," the cook replied while handing a customer a burger and fries basket.

"Has anyone reported seeing a car and trailer parked in this area for a long time?" Martin asked.

"Officers, I haven't heard anyone talking about seeing a car and trailer parked for an extended amount of time," the cook answered, putting two burgers on the grill and sighing because he was getting agitated with the police officers.

"Thank you, sir, for talking to us. We won't bother you anymore...today," Martin said as he gestured for Franklin to follow him out of the pavilion.

"I guess that car and trailer just disappeared into thin air. Do you reckon, Martin?" Franklin asked while getting into the police cruiser.

"It's got to be somewhere. It just didn't disappear. We will find it...sometime...I guess," Martin replied while starting the cruiser, leaving the pavilion, and heading for the department.

Martin thought to himself, *there is something not right, and something that we missed at the docks.*

"Martin, you okay, man?" Franklin asked, worried about the faraway look Martin had.

"What?" Martin asked Franklin.

"Yeah, I am okay. I was thinking about the boat landings and the docks. That maybe...we overlooked something."

"I'm getting a bit *hungry*. Can we stop by Jimbo's and get something to eat?" Franklin asked, rubbing his stomach and sighing.

"Sure, we can stop and get something to eat," Martin replied, looking at the large group of cars approaching in the opposite lane.

There were six cars, two sedans, four SUVs, and three pickup trucks; some were gray, and some were black, and they all had blue lights flashing. They were traveling at a high rate of speed, headed toward the lake.

"Do you think we need to go and pull them over for *speeding*, Martin?" Franklin asked, turning his head to watch them pass by.

The wind was picking up, and the trees swayed on both sides of the road. A storm was coming toward Lake Tisdale, coming in two parts: Mother Nature and the Feds.

"No, we need to leave them...alone, Franklin. They are the *Feds*, and I don't want to get into trouble with the chief and the sheriff for pulling them over for speeding."

Martin and Franklin arrive at Jimbo's Bar and Grill. As soon as they got out of the cruiser and looked toward the road, they saw more gray and black vehicles with the blue lights flashing, and behind them were the sheriff's car and several deputy sheriff vehicles.

"Wonder what the hell...is going on?" Franklin asked Martin while shaking his head as the vehicles passed the bar and grill at a high rate of speed.

"I don't know, Franklin. I *honestly*...don't know," Martin replied as he locked the cruiser and he and Franklin started walking toward the entrance to the grill.

Before they could enter the grill, the chief and assistant chief pulled up in a police cruiser at the grill and parked beside the one Martin and Franklin were in.

"Martin, Franklin, wait a minute," the chief said sternly after he rolled down the passenger window.

"What's up, chief?" Franklin asked curiously and then was distracted by a flock of geese squawking and flying overhead in a v-formation.

"The Feds got a tip from someone at the lake, that the car and trailer had been found...in the water at one of the older boat landings. The one at the far end of the lake. That hasn't been used in many years," the chief said informatively, while Mason Biggs, the assistant chief, stuck his head out of the driver-side window to watch the geese fly by overhead.

"After you two...*eat*. I want you to come back to the docks, and get with Paul Chambers. I have called Derrick and Greta; they are on their way to the docks, too."

"Okay, chief, we will get a quick burger and drink and then be on our way back to the docks," Martin replied as he looked perplexed about the find at the lake.

"Okay, we are on our way to the lake. I will contact you two...later," the chief said, raising the window back up and gesturing for the assistant chief to proceed toward the lake.

"Hmm, you were right, Martin, about your gut feelings of something not being right at the boat landing," Franklin said, holding the door open for Martin.

The storm was developing quickly, and it was beginning to rain. In the distance, thunder could be heard, and flashes of lightning could be seen. The storm was coming over the town and appeared to be headed for the lake. Gray clouds were changing to dark black, and they were moving at a fast pace.

After Martin and Franklin entered Jimbo's and ordered their burgers and fries, Greta McCall entered and walked to the counter, and Ruthie had her and Mallow's Cheeseburger Specials in a to-go box. After paying Ruthie and leaving her a generous tip, Greta looked at Franklin and Martin and said, "Looks like today is going to be busy with the Feds and the storm."

"We see you and Derrick had the same idea we did," Franklin said, smiling at Greta while Martin was ordering his and Franklin's burgers.

"Eat hearty, guys. It could be a long day," Greta said seriously as she walked out the door and to the SUV.

A few minutes later, Mallow and Greta were on their way to the docks and landings to meet the chief, the sheriff and deputies, and the Feds.

Ruthie handed Martin and Franklin their to-go boxes and told them, "Y'all be careful at the lake. When a storm comes... strange things happen around that lake."

"Thanks, Ruthie, we will," Martin said politely as he and Franklin left Jimbo's.

Just as they got into the cruiser and were backing out of the parking space, a bolt of lightning struck a tree across the street from Jimbo's. The tree broke in half, and part of it fell over on the power lines.

The lines started sparking, and within a few seconds, the power in the area was out. Jimbo's Bar and Grill was in the dark with lots of hungry customers still inside.

Martin and Franklin were startled by what happened. They made sure the road was safe to travel, and then they left in a hurry on their way to the docks and landings.

All the law enforcement department officers stopped at the main docks. The Feds wanted to make sure everyone knew what he or she had to do. They were having a meeting under one of the picnic shelters not far from the docks or landings. The picnic shelters had metal roofs, several picnic tables, and coal grills for cooking. The round poles that supported the roofs were pine, and each shelter had a dedication to a generous donor to the building of the shelters.

Eugene F. Jenkins donated the one that the officers were under.

The Feds agent in charge was Feds Agent Director Steven Carlson. He was fifty-five years old, with brown eyes and brown hair. He was tall and slender, and he never wore suits. Only slacks, knit shirts, a baseball cap, and black dress shoes. He had been an agent in the Feds for over twenty-five years.

Lonnie Moses was a young black man, only thirty-one years old. He was average built, with brown eyes and black hair. He always wore his suits to work and had been with the Feds for ten years. He was the lead agent in investigations like this one happening at Lake Tisdale.

The rain was pouring, and the storm was still lingering around the lake area. It was thundering so intensely at times, that it made the windows in the dock manager's office shake.

After everyone was under the protection of the picnic shelter, the director made them form a circle around him.

"My fellow law enforcement officers. My name is Steven Carlson, I am the Feds Agent Director in charge of this investigation now. We, as most of you already know, are investigating the deaths of the couple that were found on the pontoon a few days ago. We thought that these were going to be accidental deaths from heart attacks, but we now believe they were murdered."

"I know the weather is crappy, but we all have jobs to do. We have received good intel on the location of the missing car and boat trailer. They are in the water at the old boat landing... located at the far end of Lake Tisdale. We have a crew coming shortly to get the car and boat trailer out of the water. Then that is when we are going to work...the *hardest*. We must inspect the car and trailer carefully, and hopefully, we can find evidence that will be beneficial to this case," the director said as everyone turned to look at the big rig that just pulled into the dock and boat landing areas headed toward the old landing.

"Some of us will go to the boat landing, and some will go and investigate all the docks. We believe that there was another boat or pontoon involved in the mysterious deaths of the couple. We still don't have any information on the IDs of the man and woman. The autopsy did not give us the information we were hoping for. The DNA from the two victims...did not match any info we have on file at the federal or state level."

"Does everyone understand what you have to do? Like I said, the weather is shitty, and according to the meteorologists in the area...the storm isn't going to let up anytime soon," the director said reluctantly while coughing, sneezing, and sniffling.

Everyone nodded in agreement, and Sheriff Daniels and Chief Adams broke away from the circle, walked to the edge of the shelter, and started talking amongst themselves.

"Bruce, did it sound to you, like it did to me, that the director isn't telling us...everything he knows?" the chief asked, unsure of how honest the director was with them.

"I agree with you, Roy. I believe they are not telling us... everything," the sheriff said while watching the white caps forming on the lake in the distance.

Greta was looking all around while the director gave his speech and instructions. She looked at Mallow, sighed, and said in a whisper, "Derrick, you already knew about the involvement of another boat or pontoon. So far, these Feds haven't given us anything more than what we already...knew."

"I know, Greta. We will have to play the game and do as they say. But I still believe that the old sedan at the used car lot needs to be searched. We might find some answers there," Mallow said, disappointed about being called back to the docks and landings.

"Okay, I have written your team assignments with the help and cooperation of your senior officers, chief of police, and the sheriff of Jenkins County. We will all have important jobs to perform. So, let's get started, and see if we can narrow down what happened, and who caused it by the end of the day," the director said earnestly.

The director, after finishing with his instructions to the law enforcement group, walked over to Lonnie Moses, who was sitting at one of the picnic tables looking through his notes.

"Lonnie, I want you to check on all the groups: the local law enforcement teams, the sheriff's teams, and ours. I want to know if they find anything as soon as they do. Do you...*understand* me?" The director said vehemently.

"I will, sir." Lonnie agreed, closing his notepad before the director could see what he had written.

Martin and Franklin were on their way to the dock manager's office when a bolt of lightning hit a sailboat moored to the docks nearest to the office.

"Damn! That was close," Franklin said, wiping the rain off his face.

"*Too* close...if you ask me," Martin replied as he and Franklin picked up the pace to Paul Chamber's office.

Greta and Mallow walked out onto one of the docks, looking all around for any kind of evidence. The rain surely had washed away any significant evidence.

The rain was still pouring with no signs of letting up, and the thunder and lightning were intensifying.

"Wouldn't you think that the director would at least wait until this storm ceased before doing any full-scale investigating?" Greta asked as she sneezed several times and was breathing heavily.

"You would think that he would wait...but he didn't. It seems that there is something else he is looking for instead of the car and boat trailer. Something different entirely than what is associated with the deaths of the couple," Mallow replied while leaning down and taking a look underneath the dock.

Martin and Franklin arrived at the dock manager's office. They opened the door and Paul Chambers wasn't sitting at his desk and doing what he usually did. Playing games on the computer with the radio volume at maximum playing 'country and western' songs. He was not in his office and nowhere in sight.

"Wonder if he left because of the storm. Maybe, he's taking Saturday off?" Franklin said while Martin walked outside the office and looked at the cars parked near the docks.

Chambers drove a blue and white 'king cab,' old pickup truck to work every day and usually parked it in front of the dock near his office. The pickup was in its usual parking place. But no sign of its owner was near the premises.

"Mr. Chambers! MR. CHAMBERS!" Martin shouted, with the palms of his hands forming a circle around his mouth.

There was no reply, and the storm appeared to be settled in for the day, the mist coming toward the docks and landings from the backside of the lake.

The pouring rain soon became a monsoon, and it was hard to move around outside, you couldn't see five feet in front of you, so all the law enforcement personnel ran back under the picnic shelter.

Director Carlson sighed when he saw everyone running toward the shelter.

"I know, everyone, the weather is getting extremely bad, and the mist is coming from the lake. I have talked to Sheriff Daniels and Chief of Police Roy Adams. We have decided to call it a day, and if the weather permits...start again tomorrow morning at eight o'clock. We will meet here at the picnic shelter. We will have a brief meeting, and then we will resume our investigative assignments," the director said, while thinking to himself, *that this was a wasteful day. I need to find...it.*

He saw Lonnie Moses leaning against a support pole and gestured for him to come to him as the others dispersed.

"Lonnie, I want you to stay here at the docks. You need to keep a check on the crew that is retrieving the car and boat trailer out of the water. I want you to make sure that when it is out, no one goes into it before we get a chance…to search it, thoroughly," the director said as he watched some of the other law enforcement officers leave the docks.

"I will keep it secure, sir. Will I get some help…later? I would like to go to the motel, shower, put on some dry clothes, and get something to eat," Lonnie said while the director put his hands on his hips, looked at Lonnie, and said, "*Sure,* Lonnie, I will have you some help…soon. But don't leave until they get here."

The director looked away and then looked at Lonnie Moses with a grimace. He pointed his finger at Lonnie and started to say something, but he didn't. He only sighed, shook his head, and started running toward his vehicle.

After the director left, one of the other Fed agents walked up to Lonnie and said, "You know, Lonnie, he ain't gonna send you any help. You have to be here all night, by yourself…guarding that damn car and boat trailer."

"I know. I just wanted to see his reaction when I asked for some help…later."

The other agent walked away and got up with the other agents who were going back to the motel for the night. All the Fed agents had left Agent Lonnie Moses all by his lonesome under the picnic shelter. Waiting on the crew to retrieve the car and boat trailer out of the water, and having to endure the storm, the mist, and whatever else that might happen on this stormy and mysterious evening and night.

The sheriff had already sent his deputies back to the sheriff's department for the evening. But Chief Adams hadn't sent his officers back as yet.

He waved and gestured for them to join him and the assistant chief at one of the picnic tables. The chief wasn't too happy about what happened at the docks and landings on this stormy and mysterious day. And now the mist was making a rare evening trip across the lake and headed for town.

"I know this day has been awful. Investigating and gathering important evidence in a bad storm and pouring rain is hard. Rain that most likely washed away any evidence that was there before the storm. I appreciate everyone's cooperation. But I must say now that we will be here again in the morning…early. So, let's go home, get dry, and have some supper, and then we will have another go at it…tomorrow," the chief said with a slight smile.

"Chief, what time should we be back here…tomorrow?" Mallow asked as the others awaited the chief's answer.

"Be here at seven o'clock…in the morning, not eight. Get your breakfast before you arrive. Be ready to work hard, because we need to find answers."

The chief dismissed his officers and he and Mason Briggs left in their cruiser for the police department. Martin and Franklin left right after they did, and Mallow and Greta were headed for the SUV when they saw the old gypsy man standing at the exit to the docks and landings.

He was soaked and wet from the rain. He looked at Mallow and Greta and pointed to the mist that was becoming thicker as it continued on its path to town.

When Mallow and Greta arrived at the exit in the SUV, Greta lowered the passenger side window and asked the old man, "What is it…Mr. Miller."

The old man looked all around, wiped away the rainwater from his face, and said sternly, "He was *murdered* by 'the mist.'"

"Derrick, did you hear what Mr. Miller…said?" Greta asked

while wiping the rainwater off the door frame and frowning at the old man.

Mallow shook his head indicating that he didn't hear the old man. He told Greta, "You know that someone murdered by a weather phenomenon is *extremely* rare. I think he is just seeking attention. Why else would an old man be standing outside in weather like this."

Greta raised the window, looked straight ahead, and replied, "You are probably *right*...Derrick."

Mallow stopped by Toby's Bakery and Coffee Shop and picked up dinner for the two of them.

They didn't say much to each other on the way home. They both were in deep thought about what went on at the docks and landings today.

Also, they weren't expecting to hear Speaks's warning for them when they got home, either.

CHAPTER 6

Lucinda, Gail, and Lucinda's sister Rosemary wait in the ICU lobby for the doctor to come and tell them about Mrs. Brooks's condition.

They are becoming worried because they have been waiting patiently for three hours, and still no news from the doctor or nurses.

The hospital Lucinda's mother is in is The Dombare Medical Center. It is located only a few miles from the North Carolina-Virginia border. It is a large facility and has a Women's Unit and a Cancer Unit on campus.

Doctor Clayton McFarland is a heart specialist, and he is in charge of treating Mrs. Brooks. The doctor is fifty-five years old, tall, medium build, and bald. He has been with the hospital staff for over twenty years and is widely known as an expert in his field.

Lucinda's sister is Rosemary Andrews. She is two years older than Lucinda and lives with her husband Bill in Dombare, North Carolina. The sisters are about the same build and favor each other a lot. They have been mistaken for twins many times.

Their mother is Grace Brooks. She is eighty-two years old, five-foot-seven, slightly obese, and has been a smoker for years.

Finally, the doors to the ICU open, and Doctor McFarland walks out and starts walking toward Lucinda, Rosemary, and Gail. The gloomy look on his face tells them that the news isn't good.

"Are you the daughters of Mrs. Brooks?"

"Yes, doctor, we are," Lucinda replies with a lump in her throat, fearful of what the doctor is about to tell them.

"This is my friend and co-worker from the police department in South Carolina, Gail Stephens," Lucinda introduces Gail to the doctor as she looks at her sister and sees the tears forming in her eyes.

"Well, the news about your mother's heart isn't good. Her heart is failing, and she is lucky she is still alive. We are doing everything we can for her. But I am sorry to say…there isn't anything we can do to save her," the doctor informed them reluctantly.

All three of the women started crying, and the doctor put his hand on Lucinda's shoulder and said sincerely, "I am truly sorry, Mrs. Brooks."

Lucinda nodded, and the doctor walked back to the ICU.

Rosemary and Lucinda hugged each other, and Gail joined them.

Lucinda looked for the doctor, and before he could open the double doors to the ICU, she asked, "Can we see our mother, doctor?"

Doctor McFarland smiled slightly and said, "Yes, you can, but please only one at a time, and only for a few minutes. Your mother is very weak."

"Thank you, doctor," Lucinda said as she wiped her tears away and followed the doctor into the ICU. Probably, to see her mother alive for the last time.

Gail put her arm around Rosemary, and they both cried together while Rosemary awaited her turn to see her mother.

They could hear Lucinda crying inside the ICU, and a few minutes later, she walked outside the ICU and gestured for her sister to hurry and come see her mother because Mrs. Brooks was in her final minutes of life.

Ten minutes later, Mrs. Brooks had passed.

It's late evening at Rosemary's house. Lucinda, Rosemary, and Gail sit on the living room sofa. They are having coffee and cake. It isn't a happy occasion this evening, because tomorrow Lucinda and Rosemary have to make the arrangements for their mother's funeral.

In the living room are many family pictures of when Rosemary and Lucinda were small children. They are being pushed in a swing in the backyard by their father who died five years ago. These were happy times, and now the happy has turned to sad.

On the back wall of the living room is a large family portrait of all the Brooks together, smiling and enjoying the moment.

"Gail, honey, you need to get home to Lake Tisdale. I will be fine here with Rosemary and Bill. He will be here tomorrow, and Rosemary's kids will be here, too. Bill's been in West Virginia on business, and the kids are coming from Indiana. I will let Chief Adams know when and where the funeral will be. So, I want you to get on your way home, dear, tomorrow morning. I am so thankful that you came with me. It means a lot to me and Rosemary, Gail," Lucinda said, trying to hold back tears.

"When this ends, I will get Rosemary to take me back to Lake Tisdale. It may be a week or more. I don't know exactly, as yet," Lucinda said as she reached and hugged Gail.

"Okay, Lucinda, I will go home tomorrow. But if you need me for anything, you or Rosemary, please don't hesitate to call me," Gail said sincerely.

"We will, Gail. Thank you so much, dear," Lucinda said emotionally, wiping the tears from her eyes.

CHAPTER 7

When Mallow and Greta arrived at the apartment, they could hear Speaks chirping tumultuously inside. Mallow looked at Greta perplexed, and she looked at him the same way.

"Wonder what's wrong with Speaks," Greta asked curiously.

Mallow pulled out his key card to the apartment and had to insert it two times to get it to open the door.

He sighed, shook his head, and replied, "I don't have the slightest idea why he is chirping so."

When Mallow and Greta entered, they were alarmed because Speaks had pulled everything out of his cage: the bird feed and water container, the mat that kept the pee and poop from getting on the floor.

"That bird of yours has gone berserk, Derrick. Look at the mess he made," Greta declared while shaking her head and taking their dinner to the kitchen.

"Greta, please get our dinner ready. I will clean up the mess," Mallow said, frowning, pointing a finger at Speaks, and then shaking his head from side to side.

"Okay," Greta replied, puffing and still in disbelief about the mess the bird made while walking to the kitchen.

Mallow cleaned the mess up, and put a new mat in the cage, along with birdseed and water. Speaks was sitting on the table between the recliner and sofa. The bird's eyes were blinking rapidly, but it wasn't chirping anymore.

A few minutes later, Greta brought their dinners into the living room on a tray, and they sat down, and both exhaled heavily, and Greta said, "Finally, we get to rest a while."

Mallow turned on the TV, and the news was on. The anchor was reporting a story about a missing child in the upstate and that the wars overseas were beginning to escalate.

Halfway through their dinner, Speaks flew back into his cage, stretched out his wings, and began to speak, "Old sedan, dock manager is missing, the mist is getting stronger, and the Feds are not telling you the truth. The boat rental people are missing. *Beware* because you *two* could be…NEXT!"

After that, the bird started chirping normally and was swinging on the swing in the cage.

"Did you get all of that, Derrick?" Greta asked dubiously while taking a bite of her salad.

Mallow swallowed cola, wiped his mouth, and got up and walked to the window. He looked outside, and at the entrance to the apartments were two gray SUVs parked on each side.

"What is it, Derrick?" Greta asked while getting up and walking to the window.

"I think we are being *watched* by the…*Feds*, Greta."

"Look, there are two gray SUVs at the entrance. The lights are off, and I just saw the glow of a lighter…probably someone lighting a cigarette," Mallow said, disturbed not by the SUVs. He was disturbed about what the bird said, and now the Feds are watching him and Greta.

"Why would they be watching *us*? We haven't done anything," Greta asked.

"I may be wrong, but I don't think they are just watching us. I think they are making sure we don't leave the apartment tonight," Mallow said as he gestured for Greta to follow him to the kitchen.

Chief Roy Adams and his wife Alice are sitting on recliners in their living room, which has many pictures of family members on the walls, and pictures of former police officers and current police officers. They are having coffee and doughnuts while watching a sitcom on TV when Lucinda Brooks rings his mobile. The chief looks at Alice and sighs, and says, "It's Lucinda calling."

"Hello! Lucinda, how are you? How is your mother?" the chief asked, already knowing that Lucinda's call probably wasn't with good news about her mother's condition.

"Hello! Chief, mother passed away this evening. Her heart just gave out. The doctors did everything they could," Lucinda said emotionally, trying to hold back the tears.

"Alice and I are sorry to hear that, Lucinda. I know you loved your mother very much."

"Thank you and Mrs. Adams, chief."

"Gail is going home tomorrow. I will let everyone know when the funeral arrangements have been made. I may need a 'leave of absence' for at least a week so I can help my sister get mother's affairs in order," Lucinda said, sniffling.

"That will be fine, Lucinda. I know that we will all do our best to attend your mother's funeral. Again, we are sorry for your loss."

"Thanks. I will keep you informed, chief," Lucinda said as she looked at her sister standing beside the fireplace in the living room with her hands covering her face.

"Goodbye, Lucinda."

"Goodbye."

The chief hit "End Call" on his mobile, and his wife said, "Poor Lucinda. She is going to miss her mother."

"Yes, she will. Even though they lived far apart, they were very close," the chief said as he got up from his recliner and went to the kitchen to get a glass of tea.

"Alice, you want a glass of tea, dear?"

"Yes, please, thank you, Joe."

The chief walked into the kitchen and removed two glasses from the cabinet. He walked to the refrigerator door and filled the glasses with ice from the ice maker. As the second glass was filling with ice, he saw lights flash on the kitchen window. He looked out the window and could see two gray SUVs near the driveway of the house.

Chief Adams, after filling the glasses with tea, set them down on the kitchen counter and walked to the door that connects the kitchen with the garage. He walked out of the garage and stood near the flower bed in the front yard. One of two SUVs was now blocking the driveway.

He started to walk toward the SUVs, and when he did, two men got out and started walking toward the chief.

"Can I help you, gentlemen?" the chief asked, agitated that they were blocking his driveway.

"We're just making sure that you and your wife are safe at home, Chief Adams. We wouldn't want anyone to try to harm you or your wife, *sir*," one of the men said rudely.

"We are Feds agents, and were sent here by the *director*, sir."

"Do you have to block my driveway?" the chief asked, getting even more exasperated.

"Sorry, sir, but it's the director's orders. Any complaints must be sent directly to him, sir," one agent said harshly, with one hand inside his coat pocket and the other resting on his hip.

Chief Adams sighed, frowned, and grimaced, then he walked back into the kitchen. Picked up the two glasses of tea and returned to the living room.

"What *took* you so long, dear?" Mrs. Adams asked her husband, knowing that something was going on outside.

"Ah! We are being protected by the Feds. They have two

SUVs in front of the house, and one blocking the driveway. The agents said they were making sure we were safe," the chief replied, frustrated.

He handed his wife her tea and sat down on his recliner. He looked at the TV and then at his wife and said, "Something is going on. I don't know what, but there is no reason for the Feds agents to be keeping us from leaving our *home*. Tomorrow I am going to find out what the *hell* is going on."

"Well, let's enjoy our evening together. Tomorrow we will find the *answers*, dear," Mrs. Adams said politely and reassuringly, reaching to hold her husband's hand.

The chief smiled and agreed with his wife.

It's ten o'clock on Saturday night, and Angela Taylor is returning home from shopping at the mall in the city of Summings.

She is startled and concerned when she arrives at her home and finds two SUVs blocking the entrance to the driveway. She stopped the car on the street, let the window down, and asked, "Why are y'all here, and why is our driveway blocked?"

"Sorry, ma'am, we are just following orders from Director Carlson. He wanted the sheriff and all his deputies, the chief of police, and all of his officers protected. So, that is what we are doing, ma'am," a tall agent with a bald head and stringy beard said sternly.

"Please, can I enter my driveway, so I can get the packages out of my car?" Angela Taylor asked with a sigh and in disbelief about what was happening in front of their home.

"Move the SUV, Henry. Let the lady access her driveway."

The agent moved the SUV, and Angela Taylor slowly drove the car to the garage and parked it. She gets out, looks at the agents in the front of the house, and shakes her head. Angela wonders where Martin is and why he hasn't come to help her get the packages out of the car.

She gets out of the car, opens the back door, grabs two packages from the back seat, and starts carrying them to the side entrance of the house.

"*Martin,* I could use some... help *here,*" Angela shouted, muttering.

A few moments later, Martin comes to the door, rubbing his eyes and yawning. He shook his head and said to his wife, "Sorry, hun, I was asleep on the sofa. I didn't hear you drive up."

"Come, and get the other two packages, *please.* Did you know we have Feds protection at the front of the house? They had the driveway blocked... when I arrived."

"What? No, I didn't. What are they doing there, Angela? Did they tell you, dear?" Martin asked, concerned.

"They said they are here to protect us."

"Protect us from... what?" Martin asked, grabbing the other packages out of the car and grunting because one was heavy.

"They didn't say, Martin. They acted kinda rude when I asked them to let me get into the driveway," Angela said as she held the door open for Martin and watched what was going on at the front of the house.

"Well, let's get inside and put these items away. I could call the chief or DM, but I don't want to disturb them this... late. It was a hard and messy day at the docks today," Martin said while thinking to himself, *this doesn't make any sense... at all.*

Two hours later, Martin and Angela were sitting in the living room, having a snack and drink, watching baseball on the TV.

"Martin, look out the window and see if those agents are still there?" Angela asked curiously as she took a bite out of her ham and cheese sandwich.

Martin got up from his chair and proceeded to the front window, he slowly pulled the curtains back on one side and peeped out. The night lights on the street had the whole area illuminated. He sighed, took a sip of his drink, looked at Angela, and said reluctantly, "Yep, they are still out there. I will ask the chief about this tomorrow… morning, Angela. I don't know why they are out there, and if they are protecting the others."

"Well, they did say that they were protecting the sheriff's department deputies and Chief Adams' officers. So, I guess everyone is being protected by them… tonight," Angela said with worry.

"Let's go to bed, Angela. I got to get up early in the morning," Martin said as he walked away from the window, baffled about the Feds agents in front of their house—protecting him and Angela.

"Please, make sure the house is locked, Martin, and double-check the alarm… system, dear."

"I will. Go on to bed. I will be there… shortly," Martin said as he picked up his mobile and texted the chief about the Feds agents parked in front of the house.

But he didn't receive a reply to his text. This worried Martin, and he was concerned for Angela's safety. *What the hell is going on*? Martin thought to himself.

Mallow was leaning against the counter and Greta took a seat at the table when she entered the kitchen.

Derrick Mallow was in deep thought. He was thinking about the old sedan at the used car lot. The car with the boat trailer at the docks, that a crew the Feds hired to extract from the water. Also, the boat rentals, and the two men that worked there. And, of course, the old gypsy man.

In the back of his mind, he recalled what the bird had said to Greta and him, "*Beware* because you *two* could… be… NEXT!"

He looked out of the kitchen window at the SUVs still at the entrance to the apartments. He shook his head, smiled at Greta, and asked softly, "You ready to go to bed?"

Greta looked up at him and yawned.

"I guess that means... a *yes*," Mallow said as he leaned over to help a very tired lady out of her chair.

Then Mallow's mobile started ringing. He checked the Caller ID, and it was Chief Adams. Mallow sighed and looked at Greta standing and holding on to the table.

"It's the chief."

"Hello, chief. What's up, sir?"

"Hello, Derrick, and tell Greta Alice and I said hey. I have two things then I will let you go."

"One, did you two notice anything unusual around your apartment? Like gray SUVs blocking you from leaving?" the chief asked with slight hesitation.

"Yes, sir, we did. There are two gray SUVs at the entrance to the apartments, and they are inhibiting anyone, including Greta and me, from leaving the apartments," Mallow replied as Greta put her arm around his waist as they both looked out of the window at the SUVs.

"We have experienced the same thing... here at our house. I went outside and talked to them. One of the Feds agents said that they had orders from the director to protect the county sheriff and the sheriff's deputies... as well as the Lake Tisdale Police department officers."

"I don't think that is the real reason they are at our homes. I think there is another reason, Derrick. I just don't know what the reason is, but tomorrow I intend to find out," the chief said, agitated.

"What's the second... thing, chief?" Greta asked because Mallow had put the mobile on speaker so she could hear the conversation, too.

"Hello, Greta. Yes, the second thing is... Lucinda's mother passed away earlier today. She is going to send us the funeral arrangements. I will tell everyone that they are welcome and encouraged to attend Lucinda's mother's funeral. I know she would appreciate us... coming," the chief said, coughing, with his voice becoming hoarse.

"We will be there, chief. Lucinda is a great lady and police officer, and she is going to make a good detective. She is our fellow officer and our friend. We should all… be there for her," Greta said sluggishly and yawning several times.

"Okay, I know it's late, y'all. We will talk about this in the morning. Get some sleep. I don't think those Feds intend us any harm. I think there is something entirely different going on," the chief said.

"So, I bid you both… a good night."

"Good night, chief," Mallow and Greta said at the same time.

After ending the call, Mallow looked at Greta and said, "Let's go to bed."

As they walked out of the kitchen into the hall heading for the bedroom, arm-in-arm, Speaks was chirping loudly and then stopped when he saw Mallow and Greta. The bird started speaking, "*Beware*! *Beware*!" As they walked out of the kitchen into the hall heading for the bedroom, arm-in-arm, Speaks was chirping loudly and then stopped when he saw Mallow and Greta. The bird started speaking, "*Beware*! *Beware*!"

CHAPTER 8

The time is six o'clock on Sunday morning, and the alarm is blaring on the night table on the side that Mallow is sleeping on.

Greta wakes up and shakes Mallow and tells him to put the alarm on "Snooze."

"I am not ready to get up, yet," Greta said groggily.

Mallow reached for the button to put the alarm on "Snooze" and stopped before he pressed it.

"Greta, dear, we have to get up… Now! We have to be at the docks by seven this morning," Mallow said reluctantly.

"Crap, I am so tired from yesterday. I don't have any *energy* at all," Greta said as she slowly rose to the side of the bed with her head leaning down, her eyes closing, and her head wobbling.

"Come on, sleepy head. Let's get a move on. You can use the shower first. I will make us some coffee and toast. Now, Greta, darling, please get up."

Greta puffed, rubbed the palm of her hand through her hair, coughed, put on her slippers, and slowly wobbled to the shower.

Mallow got up, smiled, slipped on his robe and slippers, and went to the kitchen to make coffee and toast.

Then it hit him, the Feds were outside at the entrance to the apartments last night. So, he pulled back one side of the curtains in the kitchen window near the sink and looked outside. The Feds were no longer there.

"Greta, our bodyguards are gone," Mallow shouted so Greta could hear him.

After coffee and toast and after Mallow fed and watered Speaks, he and Greta left for the docks and landings. It was almost six-thirty now, and the storm had done its thing yesterday and gone elsewhere. It was cloudy and muggy on this Sunday morning.

It was six-fifty in the AM when they arrived at the shelter where they were supposed to meet the chief and the Feds Director Steven Carlson.

They were the first to arrive. No other law enforcement officers were in the vicinity of the shelter.

"Well, you reckon they decided not to do any investigating… today?" Greta said, hoping that they had.

"I don't think so, Greta. Everyone probably is just running late."

Greta looked all around and then smirked at Mallow and said, "Huh, we could have hit the 'Snooze Button' a couple of times."

Mallow looked out the driver-side window, smiled slightly, and then he reached over and kissed Greta on the cheeks and said softly, "Yes, we could have."

Ten minutes later, Chief Adams and Assistant Chief Briggs drove up and parked beside Mallow and Greta. They waved at Mallow and Greta and stayed in the cruiser. The chief and assistant chief were eating doughnuts and drinking hot coffee.

"We should have… stopped at Toby's, Derrick. A good cup of coffee and a couple of freshly baked doughnuts would be tasting good about… now."

"Are you saying my coffee isn't good?" Mallow asked curiously.

"Nope, I am just saying you need... more practice," Greta said, holding in a chuckle.

"Okay, next time you make the coffee."

"Okay, dear," Greta said, smiling and blowing him a kiss.

A few minutes later, the chief and the assistant chief got out of the cruiser and walked to one of the picnic tables under the shelter.

The chief put two green folders on the picnic table and had to quickly grab them because the wind started blowing fiercely after he put the folders down.

"Mason, go and get that rock lying on the ground and bring it over here," the chief said, sighing, shaking his head, and looking at Greta and Mallow still in the SUV and smiling slightly at him.

"Here you go...chief. One large rock to hold the folders in place, sir," Mason said with a smile, and then he started yawning.

"Whew! Thank you, Mason. I thought we were going to have to run after all these...papers."

"Well, Derrick, are we going to get out of the SUV, or are we going to just stay inside and watch the others...work?" Greta asked, looking with a long face at Mallow.

Mallow was in deep thought and didn't hear Greta. He was thinking about what the old gypsy man said yesterday and couldn't get his mind off the old sedan at Randy's used cars.

"Derrick, did you hear...me?" Greta asked sharply.

"What? I'm sorry, Greta, my mind was...elsewhere," Mallow replied, turning to see who was driving up beside them.

It was Martin and Franklin. They were in a police cruiser and were enjoying doughnuts and coffee like the chief and assistant chief earlier.

"So, are we going to get out...or not?" Greta asked, getting concerned about Mallow's behavior on this windy Sunday morning.

"Yes, let's get out and see what the chief has for us. I know you are eager to get started," Mallow said with a slight grin.

"I wouldn't be as eager if we had stopped by Toby's and got coffee and doughnuts to bring with us. Two pieces of toast don't go very far," Greta said as her stomach started growling.

Greta, Mallow, Franklin, and Martin all joined the chief and assistant chief at the picnic table.

"I know it's early, and the others won't be here until eight o'clock. The reason I wanted you all here at this time is to ask if you had Feds outside your homes all night," the chief said curiously as he slowly removed the rock and opened the top folder.

"We had Feds blocking the entrance to the apartments, chief," Mallow replied.

"They were in front of our house all night. They left this morning, early," Martin said nervously.

Franklin stood up, looked around, and then said, "Well, for some reason they weren't in front of my house. I sat outside on the porch for a good portion of the night...drinking coffee and listening to the crickets do their thing."

"That's odd. Why wouldn't they be at Franklin's home, too, chief?" Greta asked as she watched Franklin get a doughnut out of the bag in front of him on the picnic table.

Franklin smiled and offered Greta the doughnut.

"Thank you, Franklin. I am so...*hungry*."

"Chief, you think they got the car and boat trailer out of the water...last night, sir?" Mallow asked while watching Greta quickly consume the fresh glazed doughnut.

"Hmm, I wish I knew if they had gotten it out. It might answer some questions about the couple who died."

"Hopefully, the director can shed some light on this, and why we were prisoners in our own homes...last night," the chief said, fumbling through papers from the top folder.

"I have our assignments for today in these folders. It's kind of a repeat from yesterday. But this is what the director wants done."

"We aren't going to start before the rest of them get…here. I think that maybe we are going to have the same luck as we did yesterday," the chief said just before he sighed, closed the top folder, and put the rock back on top of it.

"Chief, did anyone see the dock manager yesterday?" Mallow asked as he watched Greta with her head turned to the side watching the assistant chief eat one of his doughnuts.

The assistant chief saw her licking her tongue and staring at him with hungry eyes for his last doughnut that was in the bag. He stopped eating his doughnut, picked up the bag, and handed it to Greta.

"Don't let Derrick starve you to…*death,* Greta. Get you something to eat…girl," the assistant chief said kindly with a slight chortle.

Greta smiled and nodded her head as she rapidly ate the fresh glazed doughnut.

"We never found the dock manager. We looked for him everywhere. His truck was still in its usual parking place, but no dock manager," Franklin said, sipping on his coffee.

Suddenly, a slew of law enforcement vehicles approached the docks and landings with their sirens wailing and the blue lights flashing. It was the Feds and the Jenkins County Sheriff's Department. There were ten vehicles altogether. The first to park near the picnic shelter was the SUV of Feds Director Steven Carlson.

He got out of the SUV and sighed. He looked all around with a morose frown. Things appeared to have not gone his way since yesterday.

Then he started walking to the tables where Chief Adams and the rest of the Lake Tisdale Police Department officers were sitting. When he reached the tables, he stopped and tried to smile, but it was clear he didn't have a lot to smile about—this morning.

"Good morning, everyone, I hope you got the rest you needed because today is going to be a busy one," the director said as he pulled a notepad from his shirt pocket.

It was still windy, and from the backside of the lake, the mist was thickening and beginning its travel across the lake and on toward the town. The sky was cloudy and the birds were chirping loudly in the trees nearby. There were even a few in the ceiling of the shelter who had built a nest for their young. They were chirping loudly, too.

"Good morning, Director Carlson. Most of us didn't rest well because you had our houses blocked by your agents. They said they were here to protect us. What were they protecting us from?" the chief asked as he stood and started walking over to where the director was standing.

"Please, we were only trying to keep you safe because we were informed that several townspeople were not happy with the way the investigation was going. That was the only reason we put agents at your homes. We wanted to protect you and your families," the director said, knowing that the only reason they were there was to make sure no one left their homes until they could remove the car and boat trailer from the water.

The chief sighed and walked outside of the shelter and looked up because the mist was crossing over the docks and landing now, headed toward town.

He looked around at the sheriff's deputies getting ready to start checking out the docks and landings for any other evidence that might shed some light on this strange mystery.

The director smiled slightly at the police officers, walked away, and headed toward his agents who were getting in front of the dock manager's office.

"He was lying to us, Derrick. I know it, I could tell by the way he was moving his eyes," Greta said as she stood up and walked outside where the chief was standing.

"We will figure this all out, chief. Don't worry, sir," Greta said confidently.

"I know we will, Greta. I am just afraid that the results might not be what we expect them to be."

The chief and Greta walked back to the picnic tables, and the chief delegated the tasks for today. They were to work in pairs, and half would check out the docks, and the others would check the landings for anything out of the ordinary.

When the director got to the dock manager's office, he decided to make it his office for the day since Paul Chambers wasn't anywhere to be found.

The Feds Director Steven Carlson made himself at home in the dock manager's office. He ordered his agents to come inside for a briefing before they started their morning investigations.

He mainly wanted to know why Lonnie Moses hadn't arrived yet.

"Does anyone know where Moses is?" the director asked, looking at all fifteen agents inside the cramped office.

"We haven't heard from him, sir. All we know is that he was here until the early morning. He probably is still sleeping in his hotel room off the interstate," a young lady agent said, leaning against the door.

"Well, shit! I hoped to have a report on the car and boat trailer findings. Okay, let's look again all around, and if you find anything, don't let the sheriff, his deputies, or the police chief and his officers know anything about it. Report to me as soon as you find something. Now, let's get to work. You already know what your assignments...are," the director said as he stood up and gestured for them to leave the office.

They all left the office one by one, and the director walked over to the window and thought, *I hope you found it, Moses.*

He walked outside the office and watched as the sheriff's deputies and the police chief's officers started searching the landings and docks.

The mist was getting denser, covering the lake and most of the town. The winds were still blowing briskly and the summer air was turning cold.

Mallow and Greta were on their way to the end of the first dock, and in the dense mist, they saw a shadow at the end of the dock. As they got closer, they recognized the shadow. It was the old gypsy man, Calvin Miller.

"Hello, Mr. Miller, why are you out here on this Sunday morning?" Mallow asked as Greta looked at him and frowned.

"I told you two, *yesterday,* that the dock manager was murdered by the mist. But you didn't listen to me. See that small boat floating by itself near the shore? There is a body inside it. It is the dock manager's body. I came here because I knew I had to," Miller said as he looked up at the mist and then at the small boat in the water.

"So, you think the mist murdered him?" Mallow asked.

"Yes, I do."

"Mr. Miller, exactly how did the mist murder him, sir?" Greta asked, looking at the old gypsy man suspiciously.

"The mist turns the air bad, and it's hard to breathe, and the victims of the mist suffocate, and their hearts stop suddenly," the old man said, with tears flowing down his cheeks.

"Sometimes the mist takes them and sometimes it leaves them where it murdered them. That is what it *does.* I don't know for sure, but I believe that it is looking for something, and it is things that the people have taken away. I know it doesn't make any sense, but that is what I believe, and I know I am not the only one," the old man said as he nodded his head at Mallow and Greta and started walking toward the shore.

Mallow and Greta looked at each other, perplexed about what the old man had said. Nothing about what was happening here made any sense whatsoever.

Mallow looked around, shook his head, and shouted to the

chief, "There is a body in that small boat near the shore, chief. We believe it is the dock manager Paul Chambers, sir."

The chief was talking to Sheriff Daniels and the assistant chief when he was startled by what Mallow had said.

"Okay, Derrick, we will get some people on the water and bring the boat on the shore," the chief said as he and the sheriff walked toward the shore where the boat was floating at the edge.

When Mallow and Greta got to the shore, they looked for the old man, who wasn't in sight. It was like he just disappeared.

Greta looked at Mallow, put her palm on his shoulder, and said in a calm voice, "Maybe the mist…got him, Derrick."

Mallow sighed, looked at the lake and docks again, and said, "I don't think so…not just yet, anyway."

After a few minutes, the small boat was surrounded by two boats with deputy sheriffs in them to bring the boat to shore.

The sheriff and Chief Adams radioed for the coroner and a forensics team to come to the docks.

Still standing in front of the dock manager's office was the director. He sighed, cursed, and lit up a cigarette. Then he looked at the docks, the lake, and the sheriff's deputies pulling the boat with the body to shore. He shook his head, looked up at the mist continuing to become denser, and thought to himself, *they haven't left yet*.

Twenty minutes later, the boat with the body was on the shore at the docks and landings. They were awaiting the arrival of the coroner and the forensics team.

Mallow walked over to where the chief and assistant chief were standing under the shelter talking. He stopped, sighed, and then continued walking toward them.

"Chief, I don't think we are going to find anything else here at the lake and docks, sir," Mallow said as he turned his head and looked at the boat with the body of the dock manager at the shores.

"If it is okay, sir, I want to go to Rogers Boat Rentals again. Something tells me that there might be a clue there. Greta and I could quickly drive up there, check it out, and return in an hour or so."

The chief looked at the assistant chief and then at Mallow. He sighed and reluctantly replied, "Go ahead, but make it quick. I think the director and his agents are watching us closely."

"We will make it quick, sir. I promise."

Mallow walked away and gestured for Greta to follow him to the SUV. She was still down at the shore around the boat.

A few moments later, the Coroner Christopher M. Potts and the Jenkins County Sheriff's Department forensic team arrived and parked near the picnic shelter.

Standing before the dock manager's office, Director Carlson sighed and cursed when he saw the coroner and forensic team drive up. Then he lit another cigarette and thought, *where the hell is Moses?*

He started to walk away from the office but stopped in his tracks and was perturbed when a hawk flew in front of him and landed on the roof of the office.

The hawk gawked at the director and kept walking from side to side on the roof. The bird never took his eyes off of the director.

Carlson put the cigarette out on the dock with his shoe and slowly walked away from the dock and headed toward his SUV.

The hawk watched him as he opened the door to the SUV and got in. Then the bird raised his wings, looked all around, and flew away to the back side of the lake.

The director watched as the hawk flew away. He lit another cigarette, puffed it several times, coughed, sighed, and said, "Now they are using birds to watch me."

Then he turned toward the shelter and saw Mallow and Greta getting into their SUV and leaving.

Agitated, he got out of his SUV and walked to where one of the Feds agents was standing by the dock and making notes on a brown pad.

"Where are they going?" the director asked the agent.

"They are going to the boat rentals, *sir*," the agent replied, still writing.

"I hope everything is secure there?" the Director asked, breathing rapidly and coughing, huffing, while stomping out his cigarette on the ground.

"Yes, sir! It is! Just like you requested, *sir*! We put 'Gone Out of Business' signs all around the property. All the boats, trailers, and accessories have been hauled away. The offices have been thoroughly cleaned and everything removed and taken to our warehouse in Georgia…sir," the agent replied, putting his pad and pen away in his coat pocket.

"What now, sir? Is there anything else we need to do…here?"

"One thing! Find Moses!" the director shouted, exasperated.

He turned away from the agent and headed back toward his SUV. He got in, started the engine, looked around, cursed, lit another cigarette, and drove away quickly.

CHAPTER 9

Mallow and Greta are on their way to Rogers Boat Rentals. They aren't talking to each other because Mallow is in deep thought.

Suddenly, Greta shouts, "LOOK OUT!"

Mallow swerves to avoid hitting the old gypsy man standing in the middle of the road. Mallow pulls over to the side of the road and looks straight ahead.

The old man is in a daze and doesn't move or blink an eye as the SUV almost hits him.

Greta is startled and breathing heavily. She looks at Mallow, who now looks like he is also in a daze.

"Derrick? Derrick Mallow."

"Come out of it, Derrick," Greta demands while letting the window down to shout at the old gypsy man.

"Mr. Miller, you all right?"

The old man shakes his head and turns toward the SUV and says, "You are too late. They have removed everything and the people have been murdered by the mist."

Greta gets out of the SUV, turns, looks at Mallow, sighs, and walks to where the old man is standing. The old man is trembling and panting. He looks at Greta and then at Mallow sitting in the SUV and points toward town.

"Those who aren't supposed to be here...are *gone*...now. Soon the mist will take us all. You two are good people, but you need to *leave* this town to protect...yourselves. He has already been touched by the evil that *lingers* inside the mist. Take him home now...or it will be, *too* late," the old man says to Greta as he begins walking toward town.

"Can we give you a lift, sir?" Greta asks.

The old man does not reply and Greta turns her attention back to Mallow still sitting in the SUV in a daze. Then she hears a loud noise coming from the direction the old man is walking. She turns and looks and the old man is gone.

Greta shakes her head and thinks, *what the hell is going on here?*

She walks over to the driver-side window of the SUV and taps on the glass. Mallow jumps and turns the wheel like he is still trying to swerve to keep from hitting the old man.

He finally is aware of what is happening. He lets down the window, looks at Greta, and says with a worried look on his face, "Did I hit him?"

Greta sighs, puts her hand on Mallow's shoulder, and says reassuringly, "No, you didn't hit him."

Mallow gets out of the SUV and looks at the vacant property that was Rogers Boat Rentals. He is perplexed as to why there are "Gone Out Of Business" signs all around the property boundaries.

Greta leans against the driver-side door of the SUV. She is concerned about Mallow, and about what the old man had said. This is something she never encountered before in her years as a detective.

What caused Mallow to go into the daze, and why was the old man standing in *the middle of the road,* she thought as she sighed and rubbed her palm through her hair.

A few minutes later an old pickup truck is coming down the

road. An old man is driving and a young boy is in the passenger seat. It is Arthur McKinnon and his grandson Ralph.

He slows down and stops behind the SUV. Mr. McKinnon and Ralph get out of the pickup and Arthur McKinnon says, "What's going on here, Derrick and Greta? Why has the place gone out of business? I needed some parts for my boat motor and I called Carl over a week ago and told him to order them for me. I never got a call that the parts had arrived so I thought I would drive down here and see what was going on. I had no idea they went out of business."

Mallow clears his throat and looks at Greta who is still leaning against the SUV holding her head down waiting for the answer he is going to give Mr. McKinnon.

"Honestly, Mr. McKinnon, we haven't got a clue as to why the place went out of business. The old gypsy man told Greta that the mist had murdered the people who ran the boat rentals. I know it sounds crazy, but I have no other explanation. This whole case has been baffling."

"The mist is dangerous, especially in the summertime," Ralph McKinnon says as he grabs his grandfather's hand and holds on tight.

"What do you think, Mr. McKinnon?" Greta asks curiously while shielding her eyes with her hand from the sun.

"I believe that the whole mist thing is a myth. Something the elders started rumors about many years ago. I don't think the mist that comes from the lake is killing anybody. It doesn't add up to…me. There's got to be another answer to all that has happened in the last week."

"Calvin Miller hasn't been right since his parents disappeared many years ago. He still thinks that the mist murdered them. He is a good man and a smart man, but he is troubled. He hasn't acted normal in many years," Mr. McKinnon says shaking his head and looking at his grandson.

"Well, I guess we will return to the docks, Greta. Mr. McKinnon, you and Ralph be careful, sir. We will talk later," Mallow says as he gestures for Greta to get in the car on the passenger side, but she refuses.

"No, you are not driving, mister...I am," Greta says as she returns the gesture for Mallow to get in on the passenger side of the SUV.

"Y'all better be careful, too," Mr. McKinnon says as he and Ralph return to the pickup truck and head back home.

Greta starts the SUV and smiles at Mallow who gives her a peculiar look and turns his head toward the road. Greta turns the SUV around and starts back toward the docks and landings when Mallow's mobile phone starts ringing.

It is Chief Adams on the "Caller ID."

"Derrick, you and Greta go home and get some rest. We are leaving the docks now. There's nothing else we can do here. I will see you both at the police department in the morning."

"Chief, the boat rentals were abandoned, and there were 'Gone Out Of Business' signs around the property. The entrance gate was locked, and there wasn't any information other than the signs. Nothing that would inform those who had boats and trailers rented, and had not returned them...as to what they needed to do. It was puzzling, sir," Mallow informs while rubbing his head because he is feeling depleted.

"I know, Derrick. We will find some answers...*tomorrow*...I hope," the chief replies in disbelief about what is happening in his once peaceful little town of Lake Tisdale.

CHAPTER 10

When Derrick Mallow and Greta McCall arrive at their apartment, the mist is so dense the visibility is only a couple of feet.

They get out of the SUV and slowly walk toward the door. The mist is acutely warm and wet feeling.

Birds fly around the apartment building, and squirrels jump on top of the roof as if trying to flee a predator.

The two detectives are having problems breathing because of the mist. Mallow fumbles for his keycard and drops it on the walkway.

"Damn, shit. I didn't want to do that," Mallow says holding his chest.

"I got it, Derrick. It's at my feet," Greta says as she picks up the keycard, inserts it inside the electronic lock, and exhales when the light turns green and they are able to get inside out of the mist.

"I'm glad this day is over and we are…out of that damn… mist," Mallow says as he sneezes and coughs several times.

"I have been in mist and fog before, but this mist this evening was the thickest I have ever seen. The smell was pungent, and that is not normal for mist. It was difficult to breathe, and the dampness was eerie," Greta says as she sighs, holds her head up, and exhales sharply.

"I am also glad this day is over," Greta says as she sits on the recliner, pulls off her shoes, and raises the footrest.

"I got to feed Speaks, and then I will fix us some pot pies if that is all right with you, Greta?" Mallow asks.

Greta picks up the remote and turns on the TV to the local news channel out of Columbia. She sneezes, yawns, looks up at Mallow, and says, "You feed Speaks. I am going to make us some vegetable soup using my grandmother's 'Secret Recipe.'"

"Okay, that sounds great, Greta."

Mallow gets up and puts fresh birdseed and water in the feeder for the bird, and then he sits down in the recliner, pulls his shoes off, and walks into the kitchen.

"Derrick, darling, you need to go and sit down and rest. Listen to the news. See if anything is new from the Feds or the sheriff's department. *Besides*...you look like...*shit*. You are white as a sheet."

Mallow frowns at Greta, nods, walks back into the living room, sits down in the recliner, and as soon as he does, he is sound asleep.

Speaks is busy eating his supper, and when he finishes he looks all around, flies out of the cage, and lands on the back of the recliner. He whispers into Mallow's right ear, "I told you two to be...*aware*...didn't I."

Mallow leans back in the recliner, snoring, and moving his head around, and says, "Yes, you did."

The bird flies toward the window and lands on the seal. He looks at the mist and starts prancing back and forth on the window seal, chirps loudly several times, and shouts nervously, "They're outside."

In the kitchen, Greta opens cans of veggies and browns hamburger meat in the frying pan, preparing her grandmother's vegetable soup. She has no idea what is happening outside in the dense mist.

Outside, the mist is congealing and the windows have moisture building up on them. Greta walks into the living room with a tray with two bowls of vegetable soup and puts Mallow's on the table beside his recliner.

Speaks is on the front window seal walking back and forth frantically.

Greta sets her soup on the table near the sofa and walks over to the window where the bird is, holding a cola. She looks down at the bird and then she rubs the window glass.

She jumps back from the window, drops her cola on the floor, and shouts, "Mallow! Derrick! *Come here*!"

Mallow does not respond; he is in a daze. He is muttering and making no sense at all and looking straight ahead.

Greta is startled and shaking immensely because outside she sees small figures about four feet tall with big blue glowing eyes walking all around the parking lot. They are dressed in white cloaks, and the color of their faces is teal green. The shape of their faces is elongated, and they have enormous feet.

These figures aren't trying to get into the vehicles or any of the apartments, they are just congregating. Greta keeps looking at them and she counts over a hundred of the figures.

She is flummoxed by what she is seeing. It is unbelievable, and she starts breathing rapidly. She looks back at Mallow and then returns her attention to the window and the figures outside.

Then suddenly, one of the figures approaches the window and points a finger at Greta. She freezes where she is standing, and now she is in a daze, too.

In Lake Tisdale, it is Monday morning, June 30, 2025. At the apartment where Derrick Mallow and Greta McCall live, the bird named Speaks is chirping constantly and saying, "It's six o'clock, on Monday morning, and time to get up. Everything has changed, *now*."

The alarm on the clock on the night table starts blaring, and the red LED is showing "6:00 AM." Mallow raises his head slowly and reaches for the "Alarm Silence Button." But this morning he is heavy-handed and knocks the clock on the floor. The noise of the clock falling startles Greta and she jumps out of bed breathing heavily.

"Greta, dear! It's all right, I just knocked the clock on the floor…sorry," Mallow says while yawning, getting out of bed, and stretching.

"That was a short night of sleep. Seems like I just laid down," Mallow says watching Greta put her bedroom shoes on and hurrying out of the bedroom to the living room.

"Where's the cola I dropped on the floor? *And,* where is the vegetable soup I put on the table between the recliner and sofa," Greta says perplexed and shaking her head.

Then Mallow walks into the living room and looks concerned as he watches Greta pace around the living room and look down at the floor.

She sees Mallow and frowns.

"Did you clean up the cola I spilled on the floor near the front window?" she asks Mallow while she closes her eyes and sighs.

"No! Because you didn't spill any cola by the front window, Greta. We had our supper in the kitchen. Remember, I heated two microwavable dinners for us," Mallow replies, uncertain of what is happening in Greta's head this morning.

"The mist, it was so thick, and the windows were getting fogged up with moisture on them, and the little people outside with the blue glowing eyes and red cloaks were all around the parking lot, and one was pointing…at me. You don't remember me shouting at you?" Greta asks disconcerted.

"No! I don't remember that, Greta. You probably were dreaming about this and it was so real that…you thought it happened…my dear," Mallow says trying to calm Greta down.

Speaks is chirping louder and louder, repeating the same sentence repeatedly, "Everything has changed, *now*."

Greta puts her hands over her face and shakes her head. Mallow walks over to her, puts his arms around her, and says, "It was just a dream. It wasn't real."

Greta nods and smiles slightly, "You're probably right. It was just a dream."

"Okay, I am going to make us some coffee, eggs, bacon, and toast, and you, my beautiful lady, are going to shower and get ready while I cook breakfast. And, when you are through, you can set the table, pour our coffees, and butter our toast...while I take a shower," Mallow says with a smile. Then he kisses her on the forehead and gestures for her to go to the bathroom.

After eating breakfast, and feeding Speaks, the two detectives are on their way to another day at the Lake Tisdale Police Department. However, on this day everything is different from what was yesterday.

CHAPTER 11

Monday mornings are typical in Lake Tisdale. The local stores and businesses are opening up, getting ready for the day ahead. The townspeople are walking on the sidewalks looking inside the windows of the stores and trying to decide which ones they will patronize this morning.

The police department begins its Monday with the early briefing conducted by Chief Adams and Assistant Chief Mason Briggs. The head of the Homicide Investigations Department is Derrick Mallow, and his duties are to assign the other detectives their job assignments.

In the chief's office this morning, the files that he had on his desk yesterday are not there. They have mysteriously disappeared. His desk has more files on it, but they are entirely different. These files are just normal occurrences in the town: parking violations, speeding tickets, failure to stop at stop signs, and petty theft. But no files on the recent murders. Nothing on file that has any information dealing with the association with the Feds or sheriff's department.

The chief walks in the hallway and pours himself a cup of coffee. He is getting antsy because Franklin hasn't arrived yet with the morning doughnuts. It was his turn to bring them.

Assistant Chief Briggs is in his office sitting at his desk with a perplexed expression on his face. He is thinking, *these aren't the duty details I laid out yesterday.*

"Where the hell is Franklin? I didn't have any breakfast this morning, and I was counting on having a few doughnuts with my coffee," the chief said disheartened.

"Chief, I forgot to tell you… Franklin called me early this morning and said he would be thirty minutes late. He had a flat tire on his car," Assistant Chief Briggs informed, still baffled about the files that were on his desk. He didn't have any recollection of putting them there.

The back door to the department opened, and Martin and Gail walked into the hallway headed for the receptionist's desk. They were talking about how beautiful a day it was on this particular Monday morning.

"Hello, Chief. Hello, Assistant Chief," Gail Stephens greeted as she put her purse down behind the desk and poured herself a cup of coffee.

"Hello, Gail, Martin. Welcome to another Monday morning of police work, my friends," the chief said with a chuckle as Mason Briggs walked out of his office grinning at what the chief had just said.

"Where are the doughnuts?" Martin asked, concerned because he didn't get his usual breakfast this morning. Angela had a cold and was still in bed.

"Franklin is going to be late. A flat tire on his car," the assistant chief informed.

"Well, crap. I was tasting those delicious doughnuts as Gail and I were entering the hallway, and now my taste buds are depressed," Martin said, frowning.

"Good morning, Lake Tisdale Police Department officers. I hope you are all having a good Monday morning," Greta McCall said as she and Mallow entered through the back door.

Mallow just nodded his head to everyone and yawned.

"Good morning, Derrick and Greta. Get your cups of coffee and have a seat. We are waiting on doughnuts," the assistant chief said as he poured himself another cup.

Gail Stephens stood up behind her receptionist's desk and pulled out a piece of paper.

"Hey guys, I have the day, place, and time of Lucinda's mother's funeral. It's going to be at the Baptist church in Dombare, on Tuesday at three o'clock," Gail informed.

The others looked at each other and shook their heads in disbelief. Then the chief spoke.

"When did Lucinda's mother die, Gail?"

Gail Stephens looked dumbfounded. She couldn't believe what the chief asked her.

"Chief, I was there with her the weekend, sir… remember. You let us take a cruiser to North Carolina."

The chief and the others stared at each other and then at Gail, and then the back door opened, and in stepped Franklin Stokes yelling, "I got the doughnuts."

"I don't remember anything about letting you and Lucinda take a police cruiser to North Carolina. I didn't even know her mother had passed… away," the chief said, confused.

Mallow, Mason Briggs, Martin, and Franklin were all flummoxed about what they heard from Gail. Only Greta could recall Gail and Lucinda going to North Carolina.

Greta took a sip of coffee and stared down at the floor. She looked at Gail and then Mallow and the others, and she knew that something was not right. Something with their memories had changed. She remembered what Speaks said, *everything had changed, now.*

"Well, everyone, I don't know what to say. I can't remember any of this," the chief said as he sighed, looked at Gail, and shook his head.

"Chief, I don't think you are the only one who has had a lapse of memory. I have, too. I don't remember Lucinda's mother dying, and you letting them drive a cruiser to North Carolina," Mallow said as he began thinking, *this can't be right. It can't be.*

"Mason, Martin, Franklin, Greta, do you remember?" the chief asked as he sat down in a chair and held his head down with his hand on his forehead.

"No, chief, we don't. Do you, Greta?" Martin asked curiously.

Greta looked at everyone and said, "I am not sure about... *anything* this morning."

Even though she knew that something was wrong, almost everyone else's memories had changed. She was unsure about her own, and Gail seemed to be the only one whose memory hadn't been contrived.

"Let's finish eating our doughnuts that we finally got to eat and grab another cup of coffee, and everyone come to my office," the chief said as he muttered to himself, walking to his office.

A few minutes later, everyone was crowded into the chief's office. He was going through the files on his desk but didn't recall pulling them out of the file cabinet.

The duties for the police officers were: the regular street patrol that Franklin and Gail will be on this morning. As far as the duties of the detectives, they were: to go to the pavilion and investigate the disappearance of an elderly man that one of the patrons of the pavilion reported missing. Foul play was suspected.

"Okay, today's duties are as follows: Franklin and Gail have a street patrol assignment. Mallow, you have Greta and Martin. I want y'all to go to the pavilion and investigate the disappearance of the old man. I don't have anything else at present. These are the only job assignments that are ongoing. But... I don't know, it seems like there should be more. Oh well, let's get started and see what the day brings in. It is summertime here, and anything can happen," the chief said as he closed the file folder and put a stapler on top of it.

"Ah! Chief, can I ask a question, sir?" Greta said reluctantly. Because she knew that he wouldn't recollect what she was going to ask him.

"Sure you can, Greta. What is your question?"

"At the docks, weren't we investigating several murders that were considered mysterious, sir?"

The chief frowned and looked at the others, while Mallow walked behind Greta and grabbed her arm and whispered.

"What are you saying?"

"I don't know anything about that, Greta," the chief said while putting his hands on his hips and sighing.

Greta turned and looked at Mallow, frowned, and whispered these words to Mallow, "Something isn't right, Derrick. I remember being at the docks and the boat landings over the weekend, and investigating possibly three murders, and a missing boat, trailer, and car."

"I told you, it was probably just a dream… didn't I?"

"Yes, but it wasn't a damn… *dream*."

"Well, let's get to work… people," the chief said sternly.

Greta sighed and said, "Martin, let's go to the pavilion."

"I will get the keys for the cruiser, Greta," Martin said as he picked up a set of keys for a cruiser behind the receptionist's desk.

A few minutes later, after the others left, the chief said, "Derrick, will you and Mason have a seat? We have some things to talk about. This is going to take a while."

Feds Director Steven Carlson and agent Lonnie Moses watched from a white SUV fifty yards from the police department. They saw Gail Stephens and Franklin Stokes begin their street cop duties for the day. They looked at each other and nodded.

Moments later, Greta and Martin were leaving the back

parking lot of the police department in a cruiser. They were headed for the pavilion.

"Good, that means that the memory wipe of all the police officers and detectives went as planned. Now, Lonnie, we have to go and see if the same results are at the Jenkins County Sheriff's Department," Carlson said, gesturing for Lonnie Moses to start the SUV.

Carlson smiled and lit a cigarette. He took two puffs, looked at Moses, and said, "Those little guys... know how to obliterate... don't they?"

"Yes, sir, they do," Moses replied.

"They will have some of the memories, but nothing about the murders, or the boat rentals, or that used car lot. Because, as of this day, they didn't ever... exist," Carlson said, letting the window down a little to get rid of some ashes.

Moses didn't say anything else, he just looked straight ahead, because he was afraid of the director. He knew that if he said anything against what had been done, the director would have him "murdered by the mist."

Gail Stephens and Franklin Stokes are on street patrol duty this morning. They are walking side by side on the sidewalk. They pass Ben's & Barbara's Apparel Shop. Franklin looks at Gail, lowers his head, and asks reluctantly, "Do you want to go in and say hello to Mrs. Atkins?"

She looked at him and said, "No, not now. We are on street patrol... remember. Or is your memory gone... too."

"Because we didn't remember that Lucinda's mother passed? I still don't remember you... or anyone else saying that," Franklin said, feeling strange inside, like maybe something had been taken away from him.

"Our first... customer this morning, the parking meter has

expired," Gail said as she pulled out her ticket book and started writing the citation to put on the car windshield.

"Gail, please wait a minute. That is the mayor's car. We can't give him a ticket," Franklin pleaded.

"Hmm, you remembered that... didn't you. So why didn't you remember Lucinda's mom passing."

"I don't know, Gail. I am at a loss."

Gail looked at Franklin, frowned, and tore up the parking ticket.

"He gets a break today. But tomorrow I won't be so forgiving."

"Thanks, Gail," Franklin said.

The chief sat at his desk with Mallow and Mason Briggs across from him. They were waiting to hear what the chief was going to say.

Chief Adams extended his arms, folded his hands on the desk, sighed, coughed, took a sip of coffee, cleared his throat, and said, "It seems like we are missing something. But I can't remember what it is. I didn't remember about Lucinda's mother passing, or letting them take a cruiser to North Carolina."

"Chief, I don't understand what is happening. Some things are not clear to me. I don't know about the others. But it seems like there is a void in time... to me, sir," Mallow said perplexed.

Mason Briggs sighed, looked at Mallow and the chief, and added, "I am just like the rest of you. I don't remember things either. It's like we were doing something else yesterday. But today is entirely different and what we did yesterday is irrelevant."

"Well, we will somehow work this out. Tomorrow is Lucinda's mother's funeral, and I would like for all of us to attend. We can drive two cruisers to North Carolina. I will ask Sheriff Daniels to assist while we are gone... tomorrow. I know it's going to take time to figure out what's happening here, but I think we will figure it out. That's all for now, guys. But I would like for us three to take a cruiser and drive around town, the pavilion, the lake, and the docks. Just to see what's happening... in case we have missed something," the chief said as he took another sip of coffee.

All three men were extremely flummoxed about the situation. Mallow told Greta she was probably dreaming about the events she talked about. Now, he was thinking that maybe there was something to what she was saying. But what was it?

CHAPTER 12

The pavilion is busy today. There are lots of vacationers playing video games and ordering fast food at the grill at the back of the pavilion.

Greta and Martin drive up to the parking lot in the police cruiser. There are a few people outside smoking cigarettes in the smoking area.

Martin looked around and then at Greta and said, "Well, you ready to investigate, Detective McCall?"

She frowns at Martin, opens the door, and shuts it fast. She sighs and exhales.

"Let's get this done. I am not planning on staying here long. There are other things I want to check out… while we are in the neighborhood," Greta said, agitated that she remembered things that the rest did not.

Martin opened the entrance door and gestured for Greta to enter first. She nodded her head, walked in, and proceeded to the grill. Martin followed her and wondered what she was up to because he thought they were supposed to talk to the manager first.

"Greta, why are we going here… first?"

"Because I am hungry. I want a cheeseburger, some fries, and a large cola."

Martin shook his head and said, "Okay, I will get something, too."

At the grill, Greta asked the lady at the counter, who was elderly and dressed in baggy pants and a shirt, "I am Detective McCall from the Lake Tisdale Police Department. Detective Taylor and I are here investigating the disappearance of Jacob Anderson. He is over seventy years old, bald, and of average height and build. He was last seen wearing a short-sleeved tee shirt, blue jean shorts, and flip-flops. Have you seen anyone matching that description around the pavilion or lake?"

The elderly lady looked at Greta and Martin and said rudely, "I ain't seen nobody matching that description… detectives."

"Okay, we would like to order some food if that is all right with you… ma'am," Greta said while she stared down the elderly lady.

"And, by the way, have you any information about the goings-on at the lake boat landings, the docks, and Rogers Boat Rentals?" Greta asked as Martin shook his head in disbelief.

"No, I don't. You must be new to this area, detective, because there ain't never been a Rogers Boat Rentals here at the damn lake… lady detective. What did you say your name… was?" The elderly lady answered, getting pissed with Greta.

"Now, do you two want to *order*… or *not*?" The elderly lady said, holding a pad in one hand and a pen in the other.

"I will have a cheeseburger, with fries and a large cola," Greta said, frowning at the lady.

"And you, detective?" The elderly lady asked Martin.

"I will have the same, ma'am."

Martin motioned for Greta to move away from the counter.

"What are you doing, Greta? You were interrogating that old woman. She is just an employee here," Martin said.

"Because, Martin, that woman knows something she isn't

telling us, and she lied about the boat rentals," Greta said as she looked around and then back at Martin and the old lady.

"I think something has happened to you, Greta. Just like the lady said, there isn't a Rogers Boat Rentals in Lake Tisdale. You might need to go and see a doctor," Martin suggested.

"I know what I remember, and I know that there was a boat rental here. After we are through here, that's where we are going… Martin."

"But the chief said for us to…"

"I don't care what the chief said, Martin. We are going to the boat rental place after we eat. Mainly because I know that there isn't a missing old man. But I do know that Rogers Boat Rentals did exist here at the lake," Greta said as she grabbed Martin's arm, and they went up to the counter to get their orders.

Martin sighed and pulled out his wallet. Then he looked at Greta, smiled slightly, and said, "Today it is on me, Greta."

The two detectives sat down at a table near the grill and had their lunch. The others in the pavilion stayed clear of the area where the detectives were because they sensed an uneasiness between the two detectives.

"Greta, please, let's just do our job and go. There isn't a boat rental place here."

"Martin, you are a good man. But you are wrong. Your memory has been wiped about the things that have happened here, just like the rest."

"Okay, Greta, we will go to where you think the boat rental place was, and then maybe you will be satisfied."

"Let's finish eating first," Greta said, taking a bite of her cheeseburger and gawking at the elderly lady, who was gawking at her as well.

"We going to leave the old lady a tip… aren't we?" Martin asked, putting three dollars on the table.

Greta picked up the money and handed it back to Martin and said, "Not today, my friend."

After Greta and Martin left the pavilion, the elderly lady placed a call on her mobile.

"Carlson, just thought I would let you know, that lady detective, Greta, well, her memory seems to be intact. You might get the little people to bring the mist on again and do another wipe. That lady could screw up everything here in Lake Tisdale."

"Hmm, thanks for letting… me know. Keep your eyes open," Carlson replied while lighting up another cigarette as he and Lonnie Moses pulled into the parking lot of the Jenkins County Sheriff's Department.

Greta and Martin got into the police cruiser and headed to the location that used to be Rogers Boat Rentals. Greta was driving, and when they arrived at the location, there weren't any buildings or anything in the location that was the boat rentals. It was like the place never existed.

"See, Greta, I told you," Martin said, a bit agitated at Greta.

She looked at Martin, frowned, and got out of the cruiser. Greta walked around the grounds and couldn't believe it. There was no sign that a business was once located in this acreage.

"Damn, what the hell is going… *on*? I know there was Rogers Boat Rentals here. Mallow and I were here over the weekend."

"Greta, let's go. We need to report back in. Please, Greta, can we go… *now*?" Martin pleaded.

She looked back at the car and started walking toward it when she heard a crunch under her shoe. She stepped back, and on the ground was a black leather pack. Greta picked it up and opened it. She shook her head and smiled because inside the pack were business cards that belonged to Carl Anders, the salesman at Rogers Boat Rentals.

"Yes, the proof I need," Greta said, smiling and picking up the pace to the cruiser.

"Look what I found, Martin," Greta said, invigorated about finding the leather pack.

They did not see the black SUV parked in the woods across from where they were parked.

Greta and Martin left and proceeded on their way to the police department.

Not long after they left, the black SUV pulled out and headed for the town in a hurry.

CHAPTER 13

Lonnie Moses parks the white SUV in a parking space near the entrance. He and Feds Director Steven Carlson stay in the SUV.

The weather is changing, and clouds are forming overhead. Rain and possible thunderstorms are in the forecast.

Carlson looks through his contacts and dials one of the agents.

Moses is startled when an old man knocks on the driver's side window and points to the front of the SUV.

He lets down the window slightly, and the old man smiles and says, "I am just letting you know…your lights are still on."

"Thank you, sir," Moses acknowledges.

He turns the lights off with the lever on the left-hand side of the steering wheel, while Carlson is talking to one of the agents.

"Okay, I guess we will need to send our friends to North Carolina to wipe some memories. Particularly, the lady detective, and maybe do a re-wipe of the others. Just to make sure… nobody remembers about the goings-on at the lake and landings," Carlson said, sighing as rain started beading on the windshield.

"Are we getting out, sir?"

Carlson exhaled, looked at Moses, and said as he grimaced, "No, I hate the rain, and we got to get back to our 'Operations Center.' There are things to get organized for tomorrow. We have to send a team to...what is the town, again?"

"Dombare, sir," said the agent on the phone.

"Thanks, keep watching these people. Let me know if anything changes. If for some reason their memories start coming back," the director said while lighting up a cigarette and blowing smoke toward Moses.

"Moses, start the engine...we have to return to the 'Operations Center' before dark."

Moses started the engine, and as they were backing out of the parking lot, a bird landed on the hood and gawked at them both. Then it chirped several times and crapped on the hood.

"Damn, birds," Carlson cursed, taking several puffs from his cigarette, while Moses was tuning in a radio station that broadcasted on an encrypted frequency. Now, they were not far from the Operations Center. They had traveled many miles in a very short time.

Moments later, the white SUV vanished on the highway—like it was never there.

CHAPTER 14

The chief, assistant chief, and Mallow are patrolling the town in a police cruiser. They are looking for abnormalities.

"There is something wrong here in the town of Lake Tisdale. The people, look at them. They aren't acting normally. They are walking in groups, but they aren't talking or looking at the store windows and people or vehicles passing by," the chief said, concerned.

"You are right, chief. My God, everybody is acting the same way…almost robotic," Mallow said, perplexed, remembering what Greta had said earlier that morning.

The chief looked at Mallow, who was staring out the rear window, and then at Mason Briggs. He was startled because the assistant chief was in a daze and looking straight ahead—just like the townspeople.

"Derrick, something's wrong with Mason. *Look* at him," the chief told Mallow with a worried look.

"We are going back to the police department. We have to find out what's going on…with everybody. I don't trust going to the hospital, now. They are probably the same way. We will have to deal with this on our…own…I'm afraid," the chief said, concerned about the situation with the townspeople and now the assistant chief.

"I agree, chief. I am going to try to call Greta and Martin on my mobile. We need everyone back in the department so we can figure out what to do," Mallow said while opening the contacts page on his phone and clicking on Greta's mobile number.

It rang several times and then went to voicemail. Mallow sighed and looked at the chief. Then he redialed her mobile, and the results were the same.

"Derrick, try again and again to get Gail on the mobile."

Mallow dialed Franklin's mobile and couldn't reach him, either.

He tried several times to get Gail and Franklin but had no luck.

They arrived at the police department, and the chief parked the cruiser in the back. But after he turned the engine off, the chief and Mallow were in the same daze as Mason Briggs.

The cruiser Martin Taylor is driving with Greta McCall in the passenger seat as they arrive at the police department. They park near the cruiser where the chief, assistant chief, and Derrick Mallow are still sitting in a daze.

As soon as they park, Martin holds his head down and blurts, "I'm feeling nauseous."

A few seconds later, he too is in a daze. Greta reaches and touches Martin's forehead. It is cold as ice. He isn't moving, and his eyes are staring straight ahead, and he isn't blinking.

Greta sighs, shakes her head, and gets out of the cruiser. She walks over to the other cruiser to find the others in the same daze.

"My God! What is happening in this little town?" Greta shouts, and then she hears Gail Stephens crying and pleading for help.

"Greta, help me get Franklin inside the department. He isn't coherent."

Franklin was in the same daze as the others, and on the sidewalks, people were leaning against parked cars, buildings, parking meters, and night light poles. Dazed and not blinking their eyes. They were all looking straight ahead.

The people driving the cars by some miracle were able to stop their vehicles on the street before they fell victim to the daze.

Gail was dragging Franklin with her arms under his shoulders because he couldn't move his legs. Greta grabbed Franklin on the opposite side, and they both helped him up the steps and opened the door. They sat him down in a chair at the receptionist's desk.

Both women were frazzled and had to take a few minutes to rest before they were able to continue. After thirty minutes, they had all the men inside and sitting in chairs. Their heads were still upright, and they were still staring straight ahead, not blinking or moving at all.

"What are we going to do, Greta?" Gail asked desperately.

"Everyone in town is the same way. Hell, I don't know, but the entire county, other cities and counties, or the whole state could be like this. Even the whole country or the world. To answer your question. I don't have an answer, Gail. I do know that my gut instinct is telling me that for us to get to North Carolina and get Lucinda before whoever is responsible for this gets to her first. You and I know what has been going on here, and so does Lucinda. And those responsible know that, too, I believe. We got to get to her and we have got to hide," Greta said as she put on a pot of coffee.

"I need some caffeine...bad," Greta said, trying to muster a smile for Gail.

Gail still had tears in her eyes, and she was becoming frantic.

"What if this is the end of the world?"

Greta paused, held her head down, and sighed. Then she

walked over to Gail and said calmly, "We will be okay, Gail…we will be, okay."

Gail wiped the tears away and smiled at Greta as she was handing her a cup of coffee.

"Drink, girl. It will make you feel better. It does wonders for me," Greta said as she smiled at Gail and walked to the front entrance and saw the inconceivable sight that was outside, the entire townspeople of Lake Tisdale in a daze.

Greta took a sip of coffee and thought, *why them and not us*?

CHAPTER 15

The Operations Center for the Feds in South Carolina is near the border. It is twenty miles from the Georgia, South Carolina line. The Feds own the four-hundred-acre property, one mile off the highway near I-85.

It has a massive security fence that surrounds the property. There are security cameras everywhere. At the entrance, there is a gate, and three squadrons of guards guard it for each twelve-hour shift. The building is four thousand square feet, two stories, brick walls, and brick walkways. There are privacy garages for the higher officials within the organization and special accommodations for those on "Special Assignments."

Director Steven Carlson has his main office here in one of the first-floor rooms.

There is a basement in the lower section of the building where "Top Secret" business is conducted, and where those who need to be kept away from the public are housed. The basement is large with many holding chambers, and a tunnel leads out of the operations center and onto a private road.

Assistant Director Brandon McKenzie has an office on the first floor and controls the goings-on at the center. Nothing gets by him without him knowing it.

McKenzie is forty years old, tall, medium-built, and has a mustache and beard. He wears black suits mainly to work and always wears a black hat and black shoes that he keeps shined. He follows the orders of the director and makes sure those under him follow his orders.

Lonnie Moses's office is across the hall from the director. Hollering distance for the director, who usually gives Moses a hard time every day.

The little people have their area of the operations center. They are located in the basement in a two-thousand-square-foot room. This is where they communicate with the Feds, and they are the ones who say what is happening and when it is happening.

It's Tuesday morning, and Lonnie Moses is at his desk processing reports on the computer. Brandon McKenzie walks into his office huffing and puffing.

"Lonnie, when the director arrives, you must tell him that the little people don't trust the Jenkins County Sheriff or his deputies. They will obliterate their memories as they did the townspeople and the police department."

"Why, sir, what happened?" Moses asks, rising in his chair and looking over his computer screen.

"Well, it's like this, Lonnie. One of the deputies went to the state capital and told some members of the state police about what was happening in Lake Tisdale. Because of this, the little people will have to wipe the memories of the entire state population. Hell, the little people may even have to create a mist over the whole...damn country," McKenzie said, still huffing and puffing with his hands on his hips.

McKenzie sighed, pulled his hat off, rubbed his palm through his hair, and walked out of Moses's office cussing.

Moses, now back to work on his reports, was smiling and chuckling.

The director arrives at nine o'clock, unlocks his office door, and looks across the hall at Moses sitting at his desk. He sits down at his desk and presses the messages button on the phone. He sighs, curses, and slams his fist on the desktop.

It was a message that he didn't want to hear. It was from one of the other agents. The contents of the message are related to the two women police officers. One of those who wasn't affected by the memory wipe, and the other one who was out of town when the wipe occurred. The agent's message said that the two women were going to North Carolina, where the other lady police officer was because of her mother's death. She also was aware of the goings-on at the lake, and her memory needed wiping as well.

"Moses! Bring your ass in here...this instant," the director shouted so immensely that he was heard all over the second floor.

Lonnie Moses sighed, shook his head, and thought, *what the hell does he want...now?*

Moses left his office and hurried into the director's office. He was a bit concerned by the tone of the director's voice.

"Yes, sir, what do you need...sir?" Moses said as the director gestured for him to take a seat near the desk.

"Sit down, Moses. We got to send a team to Dombare, North Carolina. We need to find and apprehend those three women. I know that the two women that are on the police force, Greta McCall and Gail Stephens, will be on their way to get Lucinda Brooks...*soon*. They are the only ones who know what's going on in Lake Tisdale. I want them put in the basement where we can get the little people to deal with them. I heard about the sheriff and his deputies; they will be dealt with accordingly," the director said, lighting up a cigarette and blowing the smoke in Moses's face.

"Now, get up off your *ass* and get the *ball* rolling. I want those women in custody by nine o'clock tonight...*understand*," the director said firmly as he puffed his cigarette and gestured for Moses to leave his office.

As Moses left the director's office, two agents passed him in the hallway, and one of the other agents remarked with a smirk, "Moses, you got to tell that damn fool that you are a human being, and you need to be treated like one."

Moses sighed and replied reluctantly, "If I do, he will send me to the little people in the basement, *too*."

Steven Carlson is in his office, smoking a cigarette, drinking coffee, and cussing when Brandon McKenzie knocks on the door.

"Come in, the door's open, McKenzie," the director snaps while inhaling smoke from the cigarette.

"I hate to perturb you, sir. But we have a guest arriving at the operations center shortly. Senator Rollings from New York, sir. I assume he heard about the leaks to the state police by the sheriff's deputy. I am afraid, sir, that this visit won't be a friendly one for us, sir," McKenzie said, standing at the door entrance.

"Well, the way things are going here today, one more negative will just put more...damn fuel on the fire, McKenzie," the director said, putting out his cigarette in the ashtray and slamming his right fist on the desk.

"McKenzie, send him to me when he arrives. Make sure Moses gets those agents on their way to North Carolina. I want to let you know that the little people will probably send out the *mist* again...later today. So, inform those who need to *know* and to *hell* with those who don't know. Mainly, the sheriff and his... *damn* deputies."

Thirty minutes have passed, and Senator Rollings's limo pulls into the Operations Center's driveway. His driver stops at the main entrance, gets out, and opens the door for the senator.

The senator is not in a good mood on this day. He does not look forward to talking with Feds Director Steven Carlson.

Senator Rollings is fifty-eight years old, obese, short, bald, and smokes a pipe. He is always dressed in gray-striped suits and vests, with gray shoes, and usually wears a gray tie.

Rollings is over the "Top Secret Organizations," the ones that could cause chaos if the word spread about certain goings-on within the nation's government.

He is an unhappy man today because of the leaks about what's happening at Lake Tisdale, particularly under the lake.

The senator thanks the driver for opening the door and gets out of the limo with a ring of smoke around his head from the heavy puffing of his pipe.

When he reaches the door where the guard is, he is greeted by McKenzie with a big smile on his face.

"Welcome, Senator Rollings. Please, sir, come on in," McKenzie said, gesturing for the senator to follow him.

"How are you today, sir?" McKenzie asked nervously.

"*How* the *hell* do you think I am, McKenzie, with all the shit that's happening because of the Fed agent. What's his name, Ruben Barker, I think? If he hadn't told the parents of the missing girl about the goings-on at the lake, then I wouldn't have to be here... now, would I?"

Ruben Barker was a young black man, tall and medium build. He had been a Fed agent for three years. When it was discovered what he had done, Barker and the parents of the girl were killed. The Feds had to get rid of Barker's body. They made it look like he was assigned to another area of the country, covering the fact that he was killed.

Before they could kill the parents, they got away and rented a car, a pontoon boat, and a trailer without giving any information on who they were. The parents were rich and paid much money to conceal their identities. They went out on the lake, and it was the mist that caused the demise of the parents. The little people made sure they didn't find the girl or them.

"I know, sir, I am sorry about all that's happened. This secret at the lake has been kept for over seventy-five years, and now everything is in danger. Still, I believe soon we will have it all in control, sir, *again*," McKenzie said reluctantly and swallowed hard, awaiting the senator's reply.

"Everything was fine until those two crooks sunk that damn boat in the middle of the lake. And when the crews removed the boat from the bottom of the lake, it had been cut in half by the little people because of the contents under the captain's console," the senator said, perturbed, and still puffing hard on his pipe.

"How much farther to Carlson's office?"

"Just four more doors down, sir," McKenzie informed, knowing that the senator was getting more and more perturbed.

"Here we are, sir."

McKenzie, weary, knocked on the door and sighed while the senator waited anxiously behind him.

"Come in, the door's open," the director vociferated.

McKenzie and the senator walked into the office, and Carlson stood up and offered his hand to the senator. The senator looked at him, disgruntled, and his hand pushed Carlson's away.

"Close the door, McKenzie. This is going to take a while, and I don't want those passing by to hear any of this conversation," the senator said vehemently while sitting down in one of the chairs in front of Carlson's desk.

When McKenzie tried to sit down, the senator looked at him and shook his head. Then he gestured for McKenzie to move to the back wall of the office. McKenzie leaned against the wall and rested his right arm on a file cabinet.

Carlson sighed, lit up another cigarette, took several puffs, and folded his hands on a file on the desk in front of him.

"Carlson, you have let things get out of *hand* here. This *secret* operation at the lake has been enduring for a long time until these past few months. First, those crooks sunk that damn boat that had *special supplies* on it for the little people. Then the parents of that girl started looking for her at the lake. Well, you know the rest. Yeah, and the dock manager had to be done away with because he saw and knew *too* much. And now, that damn deputy has made things more difficult for us. We have no choice but to let the little people wipe the memories of everyone in this state," the senator said, then pulled out his pipe, filled it with tobacco, and lit it. He watched the expressions of Carlson and McKenzie and grimaced.

"I hope you two have arranged to find those three women. There is some reason the lady detective didn't get her memory wiped. I want to have all three of them analyzed. I want to know why the obliteration did not work on the lady detective."

"Yes, sir, we have a team on the way to apprehend them now, sir," Carlson said firmly.

"Guys, I don't want this to get any worse than it is now. Do you both understand me? We made agreements with the little people many years ago, and now they are beginning to believe that we can't keep our part of the agreement. And, if that is the case, we all might end up being murdered by the mist. Damn it! Keep me informed," the senator snapped as he opened the door and walked out of the office.

"Wait, sir, I will walk you out," McKenzie shouted at the door of the office.

"I don't need you to hold my hand for me to walk out of here."

McKenzie sighed and looked back at Carlson, and Carlson chuckled and said sarcastically, "That went well, didn't it."

McKenzie exhaled and walked down the hall, while Carlson opened the file on his desk and started reading.

The Fed Director Steven Carlson put out his cigarette in the ashtray on the desk. He closed the file folder, sighed, and looked at the wall at a picture of his ex-wife and daughter. Taking a deep breath, he leaned back in the chair and closed his eyes. He thought, *I should've stayed a cop in the city*.

CHAPTER 16

It was time to get on the road. It is Tuesday morning, the day of Lucinda Brooks's mother's funeral at three o'clock at the Baptist Church in Dombare, North Carolina.

Greta looked at Gail, sighed, and stood up in front of the receptionist's desk at the police department. She put her hands on her hips and looked at the chief, the assistant chief, Martin, Franklin, and Mallow sitting near the desk, and looking straight ahead with blank expressions.

The two women were still exhausted. They didn't go home last night. They were afraid to because of what was happening. Greta locked the doors to the department. They made a bed on the floor and tried to get as much sleep as possible.

"We got to make some coffee and eat a few of those leftover doughnuts and be on our way, Gail."

"Okay, I will make the coffee, and we can have a cup to go with us," Gail said as she went to the sink in the small kitchen in the back of the department.

It was after ten o'clock and the funeral was at three. Greta knew they had no choice but to leave the men as they were. They had to get to Lucinda before the Feds did.

The day was pleasant on Tuesday, July 1, 2025. It was cool

with an overcast sky. Greta sighed as she looked around the hallway and at Gail and the men.

"Gail, we have to get a move on, girl. We need to drive Mallow's SUV. But we need to leave as soon as the coffee is ready. I hope that we are in time to get Lucinda."

Greta walked to the front window and peeked out through the blinds. It was the same as yesterday. The townspeople were still in daze mode. Standing or leaning against the street light poles, and some were sitting down on benches along the street side of the sidewalk.

The birds were chirping, and she saw two dogs running along the sidewalk, barking and growling at the dazed people. Even the dogs knew that something wasn't right in the small town of Lake Tisdale.

At ten-forty-five, Greta and Gail finally left the police department in Mallow's SUV, which was full of gas. Soon they entered the on-ramp on Interstate 95 en route to Dombare, North Carolina.

The northbound traffic on the interstate wasn't bad this morning. Greta was driving Mallow's SUV, and she set the cruise for seventy-five miles an hour.

In the back of her mind, somehow Greta knew that even though they were trying their best to get there in time to get Lucinda, the Feds would most likely get to Lucinda first.

"Damn, this coffee is good, Gail," Greta complimented.

"I found some pumpkin spice creamer in the fridge in the kitchen. It was hidden behind two bottles of cola and a carton of milk. I bet it was Franklin's. He likes pumpkin spice creamer."

"It is delicious. I haven't had pumpkin spice before," Greta said, taking another sip, looking in the rearview mirror, and watching the traffic approaching them.

Gail turned the radio on and couldn't get any reception. She tried several frequency settings, but the radio was silent.

"Is there something wrong with the radio?" she asked Greta.

"I don't think so. Try your mobile, Gail. See if you can pick up a station on it," Greta suggested, now getting concerned because the radio wasn't working, but also there was a black pickup following them closely.

"Nothing, it's like nobody's out there. I can't pick up anything. The internet isn't working *either*," Gail said nervously.

"Do you have a signal on your mobile?" Greta asked, keeping watch on the pickup that was getting closer.

"No, I don't. It's showing 'No Signal' on the home screen," Gail replied, leaning over to show Greta.

"Here, take mine and see if it has a signal."

"No, you have no signal as well," Gail said, perplexed about what was happening.

The black pickup got so close to the SUV that Greta was getting apprehensive. She looked at Gail and then at the rearview mirror. Then the pickup moved to the left lane and passed them.

Greta watched as they passed, and she couldn't see the driver because the windows were tinted. She exhaled and was relieved when the pickup passed them and was far ahead of them in a few minutes.

"Whew, I thought that truck was following us and was going to cause us trouble," Greta said, glad she was mistaken.

She looked over at Gail and smiled. Gail was yawning and rubbing her forehead. Then Greta started yawning.

"We hopefully, will be able to rest...soon, Gail. I am *sleepy*, too. But we got to get Lucinda and find a safe place to stay until...this *mess* is over."

Five minutes later, Gail was sleeping with her head leaning on the passenger side window of the SUV.

A couple of hours later, they were driving down the road that leads to the Baptist church. It was a quarter to three o'clock.

"Wake up, Gail, we're here," Greta said as she parked the SUV.

Gail woke up, still yawning and stretching. She looked at Greta and smiled slightly.

"Come on, girl, let's get inside and find a seat. From all the cars in the parking lot, I would say that there is a crowd of people for this funeral. We need to be careful because some of these people could be Fed agents," Greta said, getting out of the SUV and looking around the parking lot to make sure it was safe for them to enter the church.

Greta and Gail could hear hymns being sung as they walked up the steps to the entrance. They paused and inhaled and exhaled quickly, then Greta reached for the knob and opened the door.

The church was full; there wasn't any seating available on any of the pews. At the back of the church, there were a lot of people standing, so Greta and Gail joined them.

A few minutes later, the hymn was over and the pastor of the church, dressed in a black robe, black shirt, and white tie, stood up from his chair behind the pulpit, looked at the family, and smiled. He opened the Bible to the verses he wanted to read. He paused for a minute, turned, looked at the choir, and smiled. Then he looked at the family sitting on the front pew. He inhaled and started to speak.

"We are here today to honor the life of Grace. She was a good woman, wife, mother, and friend. She lived a good life, and she loved her children, and she had many friends. I know the family is grieving, but remember, Grace is in a better place."

The pastor spoke for over an hour. Then the choir, dressed in black robes, stood up and started to sing another hymn as everyone who was sitting joined in singing with the choir.

Greta and Gail were tired, and their voices weren't blending in well with those standing with them. Gail yawned and looked at Greta and yawned again. Greta whispered to Gail, "This will be over soon, and we can find a place to stay and rest, okay? We got to get Lucinda."

Gail nodded and started looking around the church at all the people singing along with the crowd. There were three men, two white and one black, dressed in black suits who were two pews behind the Brooks family members. They weren't singing, and they kept their eyes on Lucinda. They weren't looking around at any of the other people at all.

She leaned over and whispered to Greta, "Do you see those three men in black suits? They are gawking at Lucinda. They don't look like family or friends to me."

"Yeah, I see 'em. They could be Fed agents. We need to keep our eyes on them," Greta said while checking her pants pocket to make sure she had her pistol with her.

Thirty minutes later, the funeral service was over. It was time to go to the cemetery behind the church for the graveside service.

The family left the church first, followed by the friends. Greta and Gail caught a glimpse of Lucinda, and she saw them as she walked by. She smiled and continued walking out of the church. Greta and Gail returned the smile and then held their heads down.

The three men in black were right behind the family, and as they passed by Greta and Gail, one of the men grimaced and snarled at them.

"Well, I think we were right about them, Gail. I bet they are Fed agents, and they are here to apprehend Lucinda, and us if they get the opportunity," Greta said reluctantly. She sighed and gestured for Gail to lead the way out of the church.

When they arrived at the graveside, Lucinda, her sister, and her sister's husband were the first to sit down under the tent. The three men in black didn't sit under the tent. Two of them were standing on one side of the first row of chairs, and the other one was standing on the other side.

Greta and Gail stood behind the tent facing the back of the church.

Birds were chirping, and the flies and gnats were swarming around everyone. This Tuesday afternoon it was humid, and there wasn't any breeze blowing at all. The funeral director's distribution of paper fans was a welcome relief to help with the humid conditions.

Two dogs were running across the cemetery chasing a rabbit, barking and growling, while the pastor was trying to finish the service. After the dogs left the cemetery, the pastor jokingly said, "Thanks to the canines for ridding the cemetery of that rabbit so we can continue with this service."

The three men watched Lucinda, Greta, and Gail. One of the three men walked away from the tent and took out his mobile. He was sending a text message to Director Carlson.

"Sir, we are here at the policewoman's mother's funeral. The two women, Greta McCall and Gail Stephens are here, too. We will apprehend all three after the funeral service ends."

In the closing of the service, the pastor said, "May she Rest In Peace, amen." The rest followed with an amen, except the three men in black suits.

After everyone else made their way to pay respects to the family, Greta and Gail walked into the tent to talk to Lucinda and her family.

"Lucinda, I am so sorry for the loss of your mother," Greta said emotionally. Then she hugged Lucinda and whispered, "The Feds are here. Those three men in black suits over there. We have to try to leave as soon as possible."

Lucinda looked at her sister, then at Greta and Gail. She

started crying, grabbed Greta by the arm, and said strongly, "Why are they here, Greta? What have we done to them?"

Gail Stephens started crying. She looked at Lucinda and quietly said, "Lucinda, they are here because we know too much about what is going on in Lake Tisdale. They are here to apprehend...*us*. Like Greta said, we have to leave."

"Lucinda, what are y'all talking...about?" Rosemary asked, concerned by what she was hearing.

"Rosemary, everything will be okay. Don't worry. You need to go and be with your husband and children. Greta, Gail, and I need to leave and find somewhere to hold up for a while. I will stay in touch, darling. I love you, Rosemary. Please tell everyone that I appreciate them thinking of our Mother and our family," Lucinda said as she hugged her sister, fearful that this might be her last time.

Greta, Gail, and Lucinda walked to the SUV, and Greta watched the three men dressed in black closely. They were following them, but they weren't in a hurry. They didn't pursue the women anymore. They stopped at a black pickup truck and looked all around. They watched the women as they got into the SUV, and when the women left the church, one of the agents pulled out his mobile and called the director.

"Get in the truck. Our job is through here. The other crew will be the ones that apprehend the women," the agent on the mobile said sternly.

"Sir, the women have left the church. They are all together in the SUV that belongs to Mallow. What do you want us to do, sir?"

"Stay close; don't...leave Dombare yet. The others may need help if the women can escape...them. Keep in touch with me...every hour, understand?" Carlson said while smoking a cigarette, standing at the entrance to the Operations Center, looking out of a window.

"Yes, sir, I do."

Carlson sighed, slammed his fist against the wall, and ended the call with the agent.

"Where are we going, Greta? Do you have a safe place in mind...for us to hold up at?" Lucinda asked curiously as she looked out the passenger side window.

Greta was lying down in the back seat of the SUV, almost asleep.

"There is an old 'Bed and Breakfast' on the other side of town. I believe we can stay there and be safe," Greta replied uncertainly.

"There isn't anyone following...us. I have been watching the mirror the whole time we've been on the road. I thought those three men would grab us, but they...didn't. That's kind of puzzling to me," Lucinda said as she looked at Greta and then at Gail, who was asleep in the back seat.

"Don't worry, we will be okay," Greta said reassuringly.

She checked the rearview mirror several times and the side mirror. There wasn't much traffic on the road, and no one was following them. Greta was getting stressed out. *Why are they not pursuing us?* Greta thought.

"Poor Gail is sound asleep," Lucinda said as she thought about her mother and sister.

"Greta, I forgot to ask you. Why didn't the chief and the other men come?" Lucinda asked.

Greta looked at Lucinda with tears in her eyes and reluctantly replied, "Because they were not themselves...anymore. Something put them in a daze. The whole...damn townspeople are in a daze. Gail and I believe it has something to do with the Feds and that *damn*...mist."

Down the road, Greta and Lucinda could see the sign for Moore's Bed & Breakfast, one mile ahead.

They both exhaled at the same time. Greta looked at Lucinda

with a smile, and Lucinda reached for and tapped Gail on the shoulder.

"Wake up, sleepyhead. We are almost at the bed and breakfast."

Gail rose, yawning and stretching. She looked out the window and asked, "We haven't been followed, have we?"

"Nope, looks like those Fed agents decided to go elsewhere," Greta replied.

Five minutes later, Greta pulled into the driveway of Moore's Bed & Breakfast. After parking the SUV, Greta turned off the engine and looked at Lucinda and Gail.

"We made it, girls. I am burned out. I don't know about the two of you...but I am ready for food and a nice bed to sleep in...tonight. We will deal with tomorrow when...it arrives in the morning," Greta said as she leaned back in the SUV seat and inhaled and exhaled.

"Okay, ladies, let's go inside, get our rooms, and get something to...*eat*. I am so tired and hungry," Greta said as she opened the door and exited the SUV.

Then she looked all around to make sure they were not followed. She stretched, sighed, and smiled at Lucinda and Gail, who were out of the SUV and walking up the steps of the bed & breakfast.

Suddenly, before Greta could reach the steps, a tan and black German Shepherd dog ran across in front of her—barking and growling. Greta, startled, put her hand over her heart and breathed heavily for several seconds.

The dog stopped after it ran past her and looked at all three women, growled, barked, and snarled. Then it ran off behind the bed & breakfast.

"Greta, you all right...*girl*?" Lucinda asked, walking down the steps to check on Greta.

"Yeah, I am all right. That damn dog scared the hell out of me."

"I saw that. That dog looked like he wanted to eat you...up, girl," Lucinda said, concerned for Greta.

Gail stood on the steps panting. Then she walked down the steps and she and Lucinda put their arms around Greta, and the three women hugged and held their heads down for a while.

"Come on. We need to go inside and get our rooms, and call it a day," Lucinda said as she and Gail helped a still-startled Greta up the steps.

Moore's Bed & Breakfast is an old house, nearly a hundred years old. It has been in the Moore family for several generations. Bob and Katherine Moore own it now. Five years ago, they completely remodeled the three-story house. It has ten luxurious rooms on each floor. The outside has white vinyl siding, and large round white marble pillars that support the porch leading to the entrance. The steps are white marble as well. There are black iron rails on the sides and end of the porch.

The living room has all new furniture, sofas, chairs, and tables. The living room floor has new wood flooring. The rooms have wallpaper with a Western theme: cowboys riding horses, old Western towns, and of course a dry and desolate desert at the town's edge.

Bob and Katherine are in their fifties, and both are tall. Bob has a beard, red hair, and green eyes, and Katherine is beautiful with brown hair and blue eyes. She dresses in the latest fashions, and Bob always wears a three-piece suit when he is working at the bed & breakfast. They haven't any children.

When Greta, Lucinda, and Gail reached the door, they stopped and looked at each other, and then Greta turned the doorknob and opened the door to the bed & breakfast lobby.

Inside it was breathtaking. It was so beautiful inside and it smelled like fresh lilies.

They walked to the check-in desk holding hands. At the desk was Bob Moore, he was typing on a computer keyboard with his reading glasses down on his nose. He was watching the keyboard, and Greta, Lucinda, and Gail as they walked closer to the desk.

"Good afternoon, ladies, how may I help you?"

"We would like three rooms for a couple of days. We are from out of town and need a place to rest before...making our long trip home," Lucinda said politely.

"Hmm, I am afraid I only have one room left. There are several conferences in the city this week, and we have had an inrush of guests. The room is large on the third floor. It has three double beds...and a living room area with a large-screen TV. Will that be suitable for you three ladies?" Moore asked, looking over the top of his reading glasses.

"What do y'all think?" Lucinda asked.

"It's okay with me," Greta replied, looking at all the pictures on the walls of the past family members of the Moore family.

"It will work," Lucinda replied, turning to see what Gail was going to say.

"If y'all are *happy* with...it, then I am all in," Gail said with a smile as she looked around the lobby.

"Okay, we will take it," Greta informed Mr. Moore.

"That's great, I think you three ladies will love the room, and there is a great view of the town when it is lit up at night from the balcony," Mr. Moore said while typing on his keyboard.

After getting all the information from them, Mr. Moore gave them each a keycard to the door of room 310.

"Now, is this going to be one bill or three separate bills?" Mr. Moore asked, looking again over the top of his reading glasses.

"Just one bill, sir," Greta said, handing Mr. Moore her credit card.

"Greta, we can help pay for the room...*dear*," Lucinda said, pulling her wallet from her purse, while Gail was doing the same, still admiring all the elaborate decorations and furniture.

"No, you two won't. I got this," Greta insisted politely.

"Okay, Miss McCall, the total charge for the room, dinner, and a fabulous breakfast in the morning...is four hundred and twenty-two dollars."

Mr. Moore processed the credit card through the system while Greta, Lucinda, and Gail watched anxiously. They were ready to get a hot shower, put on clean clothes, and go to the dining room for dinner.

"Here you go, Miss McCall. Thank you, ladies, for choosing Moore's Bed & Breakfast. My name is Bob Moore. My wife Katherine and I have been running this bed & breakfast for a long time. Our family has owned and operated the bed & breakfast for over a hundred years."

"Thank you, Mr. Moore," Greta said with a smile, folding up the receipt and putting it in her purse.

"Just to let you know, dinner will start being served in one hour. Tonight's special is 'Roast Beef' as the main entrée."

"Sounds delicious," Lucinda said, gesturing to Greta and Gail to follow her to the car to get their luggage.

"Ladies, I can get one of the porters to get your luggage and bring it to your room," Mr. Moore said while picking up the intercom microphone and paging a porter.

"Thanks, Mr. Moore," Greta said with a smile as she, Lucinda, and Gail walked to the elevator.

Gail pushed the up button on the elevator control panel and smiled at Greta and Lucinda. She took another look around the lobby. When the door opened, they walked inside and all three leaned against the back wall.

"Ah! I am ready for a shower and some dinner. I hope that our trouble is behind us...now," Lucinda said while wiping the tears from her eyes and holding her head down. She was thinking about her mother, sister, and the rest of her family. She was so happy that she had good friends who wanted to make sure she was safe from the Feds.

A few moments later, the elevator doors opened and waiting to get on was an elderly couple probably going down to the dining room for dinner.

"Mmm, y'all smell that sweet aroma on this floor?" Lucinda asked while taking a deep breath to enjoy it.

"It does smell wonderful...doesn't it," Gail replied as the three ladies walked out of the elevator and down the hall to their room, number 310.

"You two may...smell the sweet aroma, but my nose is zeroed in on that roast beef cooking in the kitchen downstairs," Greta said, licking her lips and picking up the pace to the room.

"Come on...you two 'slow-pokes,' I am hungry and need a shower," Greta said.

"We smell the sweet aroma in this hallway, and the cooking of food triggers her nose. Oh well, I am ready for a shower and something to eat myself," Lucinda said chuckling.

Gail was chuckling and holding her hand over her mouth as they stopped in front of the door of room 310.

"I can hear you two. I can smell the sweet aroma, too, but the roast beef smells a whole lot better to me," Greta said giggling as she inserted the keycard into the slot on the door.

CHAPTER 17

Greta opened the door to the room, and all three women were amazed by what they saw. This room was fit for kings and queens. It was decorated from top to bottom with antiques. The three beds had brass headboards and footboards. The walls were hand-painted with scenes of the bed & breakfast from earlier times. There were pictures from the early nineteen-hundreds, of the Moore family.

"This is unbelievable. I wouldn't have believed it...if someone told me about it. A bed & breakfast this fancy," Lucinda said, looking all around.

Gail closed the door to the room, and someone started knocking. Greta, Lucinda, and Gail stopped and stared at one another. Then Greta walked toward the door and looked out through the peephole. She exhaled when she saw it was a young guy porter with their luggage on a buggy.

She slowly opened the door, and the guy looked at her strangely and said, "Ma'am, I have y'all's luggage. Is anything wrong...ma'am?"

"No, I am sorry. It's been a long day, and we are very tired. Please, bring the luggage in," Greta said, gesturing.

After the porter put their luggage in the back of the room, he walked toward the door and said politely, "I hope you ladies enjoy your stay."

"Thanks, and here's something for bringing our luggage up so soon," Greta said with a smile, handing the young man a twenty-dollar bill.

Greta closed and locked the door after he left, put her hands on her hips, and said, "Who wants to shower first?"

Lucinda and Gail looked at each other and Lucinda said, "Greta, honey. I think you need to go first, dear. You have been sweating something terrible, and I hate to say it, dear, but your deodorant quit on you hours ago."

Gail turned her head to hide a chuckle, and then all three women started laughing.

"Okay, girls. Old stinky here will go and shower first," Greta said, chuckling and grabbing a change of clothes from her luggage.

Thirty minutes later, all three women were showered and dressed in dress shirts and pants. They were eager to get to the dining room for dinner.

"Let's go, girls. I am famished," Greta said as she led the others out of the room and down the hall to the elevator.

While they were walking, Gail said, "I hope they have banana pudding for one of the desserts. I love banana pudding."

"I am sure they have it, Gail. I hope they have peach cobbler," Lucinda said, licking her lips as they stopped before the elevator.

"Okay, who's going to push the button? It ain't gonna open unless one of us presses the down button," Lucinda said, standing behind Gail and Greta.

"I will," Greta said as she pressed the button and backed up a step.

When the door opened, there were two strange men dressed in black suits, shirts, ties, shoes, and derby hats. They were elderly, and one was black and the other white. They tipped their hats at the ladies, and the black man said, "Good afternoon, ladies." He walked out of the elevator while the other one was holding the door open.

"Thank you, sir," Greta said, watching the men as they walked away from the elevator.

"Do you think that they are here for the conference?" Lucinda asked, worried that they could be Feds.

"I don't know, Lucinda. But I know one thing we ain't gonna worry about now. We are gonna enjoy our dinner, and then we are going to get some rest," Greta said as she grabbed the rail when the door closed and the elevator started descending.

"I don't think they were Feds. One of those guys had a cross necklace around his neck. I believe they must be here for the conference," Gail said hesitantly as the elevator stopped on the first floor.

The door opened, and they walked out together. They stopped in the hallway and looked around. Everything looked safe, and they eagerly walked into the dining room across the hall.

The dining room was full of guests enjoying their dinner. Almost everyone was dressed casually, except for a few men with three-piece suits.

A waiter dressed in a white coat, black shirt, white tie, and black pants greeted them as they walked in.

"Good evening, ladies. We have roast beef tonight and an assortment of meats, veggies, salads, and desserts. I assume a table for three?" the waiter asked, gesturing for the ladies to follow him.

"Yes, please," Greta said politely.

The dining room was mostly quiet. Most guests were busy eating and very few were having ongoing conversations.

The waiter pointed to a table for three, and Lucinda and Gail sat down. Greta stopped momentarily to check out the guests to make sure no one looked like they could be Feds. She believed that everything was safe and sat down.

"What's wrong, Greta?" Lucinda asked as Gail was looking at the menu.

"I guess I am just being overcautious, but something tells me that this place may be too good to be true…you know," Greta replied reluctantly.

"Okay, ladies, what will you have to drink?" the waiter asked, holding a pad in one hand and a pen in the other.

"I just want a sweet iced tea," Gail said.

"Hmm, I will have the same," Lucinda said.

"The same for me," Greta said, taking another look around the dining room and then glancing at the menu that was in front of her on the table.

"Okay, three sweet teas will be here shortly. Please, let me know when you are ready to order dinner. My name is Lewis," the waiter said as he smiled and walked toward the kitchen in the back of the dining room.

"The food smells so good. And I am so…damn *hungry*…and sleepy," Greta said, leaning back in her chair and then yawning.

"We will be eating soon, Greta," Lucinda said, flipping the menu to the salad section.

"Hmm, Greek salad with any choice of meats: chicken, turkey, ham, and beef. Well, that sounds good. I think I will order the Greek salad with grilled chicken before I get my main course," Lucinda said, continuing to flip through the menu.

A few minutes later, the waiter Lewis brought them their sweet iced teas.

"Okay, ladies. We have three sweet iced teas here. Are you ready to order now?" Lewis said, ready with his pad and pencil to write down the orders.

Lucinda ordered first while Greta and Gail continued looking over the menu.

"I want the roast beef special…with mashed potatoes and gravy, green beans, and fried okra. I also want a Greek salad with grilled chicken before I get the main course," Lucinda said, folding the menu and handing it back to Lewis.

"Hmm, I guess I will have the same as Lucinda," Gail said.

Greta looked one final time at the menu, sighed, exhaled, and said, "I will have the same as the other two."

"Very well, ladies. Your orders will be ready shortly."

"Well, isn't this place marvelous?" Gail said, smiling and looking at the lusciously decorated dining room.

"Yes, it's quite nice," Lucinda replied, taking a big swallow of tea.

"What do you think, Greta?" Lucinda asked curiously.

"It's nice, and the scenery is beautiful. But I am still a bit uncertain about what might happen later. I am hoping that we will be safe here, but I am starting to feel uneasy about it," Greta said reluctantly.

Leaning against the counter that had the beverages on it, were Bob and Katherine Moore. They were talking and looking around at the guests.

"Bob, is that the three women the Feds told us about?" Katherine asked while slightly pointing at the table where Greta, Gail, and Lucinda were sitting.

"Yes, dear, they are the ones."

"So, are we going to do what the Feds said, or are we going to ignore what they said, and not help them?" Katherine asked while watching Bob's expression.

"I don't want to turn those ladies into the Feds. But the Feds made it clear if we don't help them, we would live to regret it," Bob replied, sighing and shaking his head.

Bob and Katherine walked out of the dining room and back to the manager's office behind the check-in counter.

After eating their dinner and their dessert, and leaving Lewis a nice tip, Greta, Lucinda, and Gail got three sweet iced teas to go and returned to their room.

Greta continued to be on the alert, looking around and watching all the people they passed by on their way to the room.

They all three lay down on their beds when they entered the room. They were full from their delicious dinner, and they were extremely enervated.

"That was the best dinner I have had in a *long*...while," Lucinda said with her eyes closed and slowly falling asleep.

"I agree, Lucinda. It was a great dinner and I particularly loved the banana pudding," Gail said, closing her eyes as well.

Greta just lay in bed thinking and hoping this night would be safe, and they wouldn't have to worry about the Feds, and the goings on in Lake Tisdale, and especially that damn mist.

It was after nine o'clock, and outside the wind was picking up, clouds forming in the nighttime sky.

Soon, all three women were sleeping. Greta was dreaming about being out on a date with Derrick Mallow, and Gail Stephens was having a nightmare about being inside a strange room surrounded by aliens. Lucinda was talking in her sleep. She was dreaming about her mother and the good times they had together.

Then, suddenly, they were awakened by a knock on the door. Greta got up out of bed, stretching and yawning. She looked at Lucinda and Gail and said softly, "I will see who it is."

Standing outside the door was Katherine Moore. She was holding a white box about the size of a shoebox.

"It's Mrs. Moore," Greta said as she unlocked the door and opened it, still yawning and half asleep.

"I am sorry to disturb you, but I just remembered I didn't give y'all our 'Welcome to the Bed & Breakfast Box of Treats.' It is something we give all the guests. I guess it slipped my husband's mind," Mrs. Moore said reluctantly, knowing that Lonnie Moses and the two elderly men wearing derby hats and dressed in black suits who were accompanying him were standing to the side of the door where Greta couldn't see them.

"Well, thank you, Mrs. Moore. You could've waited until morning," Greta said.

Katherine Moore handed the box to Greta and moved away from the door. Greta looked at her strangely. *Why was she acting this way*, Greta thought.

Greta shook her hand, rubbed her hand through her hair, and said, "Thank you and goodnight, Mrs. Moore."

She closed the door and walked over to the dresser in the middle of the room. Then she set the box down on top of it and started to walk toward her bed. When the box mysteriously opened, a white mist came out of it, and completely covered the room.

It only took a couple of minutes for the mist to take effect. The women were all in a daze now. Greta was standing near her bed, and Lucinda and Gail were sitting up in their beds.

Lonnie Moses, dressed in a blue shirt with blue jeans, opened the door, and with the assistance of the two men, they each grabbed one of the women and escorted them out of the room and to the elevator.

A few minutes later, they loaded the three dazed women in a black SUV and headed for South Carolina on their way to the Operations Center.

Moses was driving the SUV with the three women, and the two elderly men were following them in a black king cab pickup truck.

Lonnie Moses looked in the rearview mirror at Greta, Lucinda, and Gail. He sighed, shook his head, and said emotionally, "I hate my job."

CHAPTER 18

Today is Thursday, July 3. Lonnie Moses was supposed to have arrived with Greta McCall, Lucinda Brooks, and Gail Stephens yesterday. But it hasn't happened.

In his office, wondering what has happened to Moses, is the Feds Director Steven Carlson. He is looking at files as he sits uneasily in his chair. He has one cigarette in his mouth and two burning in the ashtray.

There is a knock on his office door. Carlson pauses, looking at the files, raises his head, and says angrily, "Come in!"

The door opens, and it is one of the new secretaries, just recently hired at the Operations Center.

"I am sorry to bother you, *sir*. I was told to let you know that Senator Rollings will be here at one o'clock, sir. And by the way, sir, you are not supposed to be smoking in the offices. Have you seen the signs, *sir*?" The new young secretary Barbara Lenny said, not knowing that the director wasn't in the greatest of moods on this Thursday.

"What is your name...young lady?" the director asked rudely.

"Ah! My name is Barbara Lenny, sir. I am one of the new hires."

"*Well*, Barbara Lenny, I am the director here, and I will smoke when I want to. Do you understand...me?"

"Ah! Ah! Yes, sir, sorry, sir," the secretary said nervously as she quickly left the director's office and walked quickly down the hall to the secretaries' offices, mumbling to herself.

"With everything going on...here, and the damn senator on his way, and now I have to be told the rules of the complex by a young newly hired secretary. Damn it!"

Just when the director got up and started pounding on the file cabinets behind his desk, the door opened, and in walked Brandon McKenzie.

"Good morning, Director Carlson, I just wanted to make sure you knew that the senator was coming today, sir."

The director turned around, grimacing at McKenzie. He started breathing heavily, lowered his head, and started huffing and puffing.

"Sit down, McKenzie. Yes, I know the senator is coming today. Now, can you tell me where the hell Moses is with those three women?"

McKenzie took a seat, and the director walked around to the other side of the desk and leaned against the desk next to McKenzie. He looked down at him still with a grimace.

"Let me tell you something...*McKenzie*. Things are gonna get tough here in a little while. I need to know if I can *count* on you...or *not*," the director said harshly.

"Sir, you can count on me, sir. I won't let you down," McKenzie replied, looking away from the director and staring at the file cabinets.

"Good, because ain't no telling what that *damn* senator is going to want from us. You do know that they plan to obliterate the memories of everyone in the whole damn *state*...don't you? Tomorrow, I think, is when it is supposed to happen," the director said, walking back to his chair, sitting down, and lighting up another cigarette.

"With the mist, sir?" McKenzie asked.

"I don't know how they are going to do it. I guess it will be the damn mist."

"The senator will probably have all the answers for us when his *worthless* ass gets here," the director said, disgruntled, and thinking, *I wish that damn mist would murder the senator.*

McKenzie stood up, exhaled hard, and started walking to the door. He looked back at the director, thought for a second, and said reluctantly, "I will let you know when the senator arrives, sir."

He closed the door behind him, shaking his head as he walked to his office because he knew that a good day at the center could become bad expeditiously when the senator arrived.

It is one o'clock, and Senator Rollings has just entered the Operations Center with his pipe leaving a trail of smoke behind him. The senator is in a better mood than on his last visit.

Mainly, because tomorrow is the Fourth of July, and the day the "little people" obliterate everyone in South Carolina. He knows when this is done, his troubles will cease to exist, or at least that is what he believes.

He passes one of the new secretaries, smiles, and politely says, "Hello."

The secretary, dressed in a navy blue suit and pants, lowers her head, smiles, and returns the greeting.

McKenzie was sitting at his desk with the office door open when the senator walked by. McKenzie sighed, put his hand over his forehead, and thought, *here we go...again.*

"Senator! Senator! Please wait on me...sir."

He didn't pay McKenzie any attention. The senator was whistling, grinning, and exhaling enormous smoke. It resembled an old steam locomotive going at full speed on the railroad tracks.

McKenzie ran to catch up with the senator, and when the senator saw him, he just grunted, sighed, and coughed.

"I need to announce your arrival...Senator Rollings. The director is very busy today," McKenzie said apprehensively, knowing he was lying.

"McKenzie, shut the *hell* up. It would help if you didn't announce me. I will go as I please inside the center. *Because* I am the main damn reason...this place...*exists*."

When the senator arrived at the director's office, he didn't knock on the door, he opened it and walked in, while McKenzie was becoming a nervous wreck walking in behind him.

"Good evening, Senator Rollings," Director Carlson said while looking at some files on his desk.

"You know...Carlson, today is actually a good day. But tomorrow will be better...we...I mean, the little people are going to obliterate this entire state's population," the senator said with a wide smile as he sat down and gestured for McKenzie to do the same.

McKenzie finally sat down in a chair next to the senator. He kept looking at the senator and the director. McKenzie knew that soon the fireworks would come.

"So, senator, the little people are going to use the mist to wipe out the people's memories, sir?" the director asked as he pulled out another cigarette from the pack on his desk and lit it.

"Well, tomorrow the weather people say that there is a one hundred percent chance of rain. So, to ensure nothing is suspicious, the little people will add a few ingredients to the raindrops. It would cause concern if the mist would cover the whole state and not any other states on our borders. Don't you think that is the best way...*director*?" the senator asked while taking a big puff of his pipe.

"It's fine with me, sir. My question is, what do you want us to do?" the director asked curiously.

"I want you to make sure that the Jenkins County Sheriff's Department has lost all their memories...first. Then please ensure that the Lake Tisdale Police Department doesn't remember anything...either. Go to each place and take this nervous asshole McKenzie with you. Act casually and don't tell them you are testing their memories. Also, I want to know when Moses gets here with those three women. I want them tested as soon as they arrive. You understand me...Carlson?" the senator said, wiping his sweaty forehead with a handkerchief and rubbing his bald head.

"Okay, senator. I think we can handle that."

McKenzie exhaled, held his forefinger on his right hand, and said, "Senator Rollings...Moses is running late in arriving here...sir. We don't know where he is or what happened to him."

The director sighed, looked up at the ceiling, and started to cuss but stopped.

At that moment, the good mood the senator was in turned to shit. He put his pipe down on top of the desk, grunted, and leaned over to talk to the director at a close distance.

"You make sure...no matter *what*...that you and your people get Moses and those damn women here by tomorrow night, or you both may have your memories obliterated, *too*. Do you *understand* me...Carlson?"

"We will find them, sir," the director replied, looking at McKenzie.

"YOU! Damn right you will find them," the senator said as he picked up his pipe, stood up, looked at the director, and then turned and looked at McKenzie. Then he dumped the ashes from his pipe on the director's desk, huffed and puffed, and said, "These ashes could be what's left of your memories...if you don't do as I say."

He put his pipe in his coat pocket, walked out of the director's office headed for the exit muttering to himself. Then he stopped and turned around and said, "Remember to wear your special ponchos tomorrow."

"Hmm, just another wonderful day at the Operations Center...McKenzie, ain't it," the director said, putting out his cigarette in the ashtray.

McKenzie nodded, stood up, didn't say a word as he walked out of the office, and slowly closed the door.

CHAPTER 19

It's the Fourth of July, and there is loud rumbling all around on this holiday. But it's not the fireworks rumbling; it is thunder. A severe storm has developed over South Carolina and Lake Tisdale. Lightning is flashing brightly in the distance, and the rain is starting. It's going to be a stormy and wet holiday.

Today is the day of the obliteration of memories of everyone in the state. The little people have mixed something in the rain to perform the task that the mist has done in the past.

Fed Director Steven Carlson has just parked his car in the Operations Center car garage. He slowly opens the door, puts on his special poncho, and inhales carefully. He doesn't want to inhale whatever the little people have mixed in the air with the rain.

He exhales, coughs, and grunts as he gets out of his SUV and lights up a cigarette.

The director sighs when he sees Assistant Director Brandon McKenzie pull into the parking space by his SUV. McKenzie gets out of his car singing and smiling.

"Good morning, Director Carlson, how are you on this fine day, sir?"

"I am alive, and so far I still have my memory, McKenzie. From the way you are acting this morning, I can't say the same for you," the director said, taking a strong draw from his cigarette.

"I am just happy that after today, sir, we won't have to worry about the little people's secret at that lake anymore."

"Hopefully, that will be the case, McKenzie. But don't bank on it. Because it's the Fourth of July, and anything can happen. That stuff in the rain the little people conjured up may not wipe everyone's memory."

As they start walking to the entrance door to the center, McKenzie starts coughing rapidly and starts to pant.

The director grabs McKenzie and holds him. McKenzie is hyperventilating. He can't stand up anymore, and the director hasn't any choice but to slowly let him fall to the floor.

"*Damn,* McKenzie, what the *hell* is *wrong* with you?" the director asked nervously as he put his cigarette out on the concrete floor leading to the building entrance.

McKenzie holds his head down and covers his face with the palms of his hands. Director Carlson kneels by him, still holding him. McKenzie slowly raises his head and looks at the director while he is wobbling from side to side.

He squints, grimaces, and then starts to fall backward. The director slowly lays him down on the floor. McKenzie grabbed the director's arm, pulled himself up toward him slowly, and said, "*Who* are you, sir?"

The director sighed and started cursing, "Damn! McKenzie, you got obliterated. Shit...shit...shit. I can't believe this. This can't be happening. You crazy fool...you didn't do as you were told. They said to wear the special poncho to keep the rain off your head, and it would protect you from the agent that contaminated the air."

"Poncho...rain...*poncho...rain.* He! He! You are *funny,* sir," McKenzie said, chuckling, and then falling asleep.

"Damn." The director said as he pulled McKenzie up and put

him over his shoulder, and they went inside the Operations Center. He sat McKenzie down on a sofa in the lobby and started walking to his office.

When he opened his office door, he was shocked. Senator Rollings was sitting in the director's chair in a daze with his pipe in his mouth, barely with the smoke from it rising to the ceiling.

The director couldn't help himself; he chuckled and rubbed the palm of his hand through his hair. He sat down in one of the chairs in front of his desk, picked up the phone, and called for his secretary, but there was no answer. No one else had made it to the Operations Center this Friday morning, the Fourth of July.

"You were supposed to be one of their advocates...Senator Rollings. You must have pissed off some of those little people," the director said, taking a puff from his cigarette.

A few minutes later, the director started grunting, coughing, and gagging. He could barely breathe. Everything was getting out of focus, and then he couldn't hold his head up any longer. He sat down in a chair in front of his desk and slowly laid his head on the desk, and seconds later, he was out cold.

It's ten o'clock at the Lake Tisdale Police Department. Chief Adams, Assistant Chief Briggs, Martin, Franklin, and Derrick Mallow were coming out of the daze that they had been in for several days.

The thunder was rumbling outside, the rain pouring, and lightning flashing and striking near the small town. The air was filled with the agent that the little people put into the rain to obliterate the memories.

Mallow slowly started looking around. His eyes were barely open. He couldn't stand up; he was weak, and his stomach felt like it was filled with cement. He could move his arms, but not his legs. He saw the others starting to awake from the long daze.

But he couldn't recollect who they were. He was with

strangers, in a strange place, where he thought he wasn't supposed to be.

The chief, the assistant chief, Martin, and Franklin looked at each other strangely. Their memories were obliterated. They didn't know who they were or who was in the department with them.

Mallow started to get feeling in his legs and could finally stand up. He knew he had to leave this place and go outside to find out what happened. He slightly remembered he should be in Decreston, New York. This place wasn't where he was supposed to be, or that's what he was thinking.

When he reached the door, he looked around at the others, shook his head, and thought, *who are you, people*?

Cautiously, he opened the door and walked outside, and lightning popped across the street. It had hit a lightning rod on the top of Ben's and Barbara's Apparel Shop.

The streets were clear; no one was walking on the sidewalks or shopping in the stores. One reason was it was a holiday; the other reason was the monsoon falling and the stormy conditions.

Derrick Mallow was in a place strange to him, and he didn't know why he was there. But, he did suddenly start to remember a little something about the people of this town and that they were not acting normal.

He pulled his coat up around his neck to keep the rain from wetting his shirt. He started down the steps of the police department, looking all around.

In the distance, an old man was walking down the sidewalk dressed in a bright orange shirt and white pants. He was looking at Mallow, who was standing in front of the police department.

When he reached Mallow, he sighed and exhaled hard. Mallow looked at him, squinted, and shook his head because he thought he was hallucinating.

"You are not...hallucinating, my friend. I am real. I dressed this way so you would be able to see me. My name is Calvin Miller. You know me as the 'old gypsy man.'"

Mallow wiped his eyes and took a second look at the old man.

"I am sorry...sir. I do not know you," Mallow said while feeling apprehensive.

The old man chuckled and looked at the smoke coming from the lightning rod on the roof of the apparel shop. Then he held his head down and said, "Of course...you don't...son. The little people have wiped your memory."

Mallow turned his head and looked at the lightning rod on the roof, and for a second, he had a flashback of spending time with Greta at the lake. He coughed, panted, and started feeling sick. Then he looked at the old man, and he sat down on the bottom steps of the police department.

The old man joined him and sat down beside him.

"What are you talking about...old man?" Mallow asked, feeling like he had lost his best friend and didn't know what had happened to them.

"You don't need to be concerned about your lost memory... detective. It will slowly return to you. You need to be concerned about finding the woman you love and your friends. The others in the police department will be...okay. But the women are in grave danger. You must return to your apartment at the Lake Tisdale Resort Apartments, number 12, and for one thing feed and water Speaks. For the other, you must listen to Speaks; he will help you understand what to do," the old gypsy man said with a smile. He put his hand on Mallow's shoulder and then disappeared.

The old man didn't lose his memory. Why didn't...he? Maybe he was immune to the methods the little people used, Mallow thought.

"What, where did he go? Hmm, just a hallucination, or I am not fully awake yet," Mallow said, sitting on the steps, soaked from the rain.

Then he had another flashback about being with Greta and the others at Toby's Bakery and Coffee Shop. They were having breakfast and telling jokes. Mallow smiled because he was beginning to remember her more.

He stood up, sighed, and thought, *I am going to need a car. It might as well be a police cruiser.*

A few minutes later, he was in a police cruiser headed for the Lake Tisdale Resort Apartments. It was time to feed Speaks and have a chat.

When he arrived, he parked the cruiser in front of the apartment and sat inside. With most of his memory wiped, he could only recall certain memories. Most of them were with Greta and his friends at the Lake Tisdale Police Department.

"So this is where I live, according to the old man," Mallow said after turning the engine off and opening the door. When he got out of the cruiser, he looked around. The apartment parking lot was full of cars and pickup trucks. But there was no one outside, and he didn't see any children outside playing.

It was half past noon. The rain had stopped, and the sky was beginning to clear. Mallow walked to the door of his apartment and saw that the lock needed a keycard. He sighed and then pulled his wallet from the back pocket of his pants. He unfolded it, and in the first compartment in the wallet was the keycard. He took in a deep breath and inserted the card in the door lock. The light turned from red to green, and he opened the door, and inside, Speaks was chirping loudly, and Mallow thought that he heard the bird curse.

"The old man told me...your name is Speaks. Is that your name...bird?"

The bird flew over toward the door and landed on Mallow's right shoulder. He flapped his wings several times, looked at Mallow, and said roughly, "My name is Speaks. I am not an ordinary bird. You will soon remember everything...Derrick Mallow."

Then Mallow sat down in the recliner with the bird still on his shoulder. On the table next to the recliner, he saw a picture of Greta, Chief Adams, Assistant Chief Briggs, Lucinda, Gail, Martin, and Franklin. The picture was taken when Greta got her detective badge and gun.

Speaks looked at the picture, and then at Mallow, and said, "Good, you are remembering."

"I hope you remember where my food is because I am starving. When I eat...then I will tell you what to do to find the three women...Mallow," Speaks said, pointing to the kitchen with his wing.

Mallow chuckled, got up, and walked into the kitchen, and there he saw on the counter next to the sink was a box of birdseed. He picked it up, grabbed a glass from the cabinet, and filled it with water.

He walked into the living room and filled the small bowls in the cage with food and water.

Speaks flew off of Mallow's shoulder and entered the cage and commenced eating all the birdseed in the bowl and drinking almost all of the water. Mallow sat down in the recliner and put the box of birdseed on the table while watching the bird eat.

"Mmm, thanks, Mallow...that was delicious," Speaks said after finishing his meal.

Mallow smiled and laughed slightly, and said, "You are welcome, Speaks."

"Okay, your belly is full of birdseed now. Are you going to tell me how to find Greta, Lucinda, and Gail?"

"*Patience,* Mallow, patience," the bird replied.

"For now, they are safe. But they won't be for long. They were supposed to be delivered to the Operations Center near the Georgia border, but something happened while Moses and the two elderly men were escorting them. They never arrived at the center."

"What happened?" Mallow asked perturbed.

"That, we don't know," Speaks replied reluctantly.

"May I ask...what do you mean by...*we*?"

"By now...you realize I am not an ordinary bird. Don't you?" Speaks said while flying and landing on the table near the recliner.

"Yeah! I know you are not an ordinary bird. May I ask what kind of bird are you?" Mallow said, hoping the bird was going to tell him the truth.

"I am from another world. My people were sent here to keep the little people, as the folks around here call them, from taking over your world and making the people of Earth their servants."

Then Speaks changed from a bird into his true form. He turned into a small blue man about four feet tall. His face was blue, his eyes, and his ears were extremely large. On his head was a square cap, and his clothes and shoes were blue as he was.

Now, he was standing in front of the recliner, looking at Mallow.

Mallow was dumbfounded by the transformation of his bird Speaks into the small blue man.

"So, tell me, what is your real name?" Mallow asked curiously.

The blue man looked at Mallow, chuckled, and said, "My real name is Speaks. You named me Speaks because that is the name I put into your head...Detective Derrick Mallow."

Mallow sighed, rubbed the palm of his hand through his hair, and told Speaks to sit down in the other recliner to the right of the table.

"Tell me this, Speaks. Where are the rest of you?"

"The little people killed a lot of us. There aren't many of us left. We have failed your world and your people. I am sorry for that. Derrick, you are a special human. You have a gift when it comes to solving mysteries. You are your world's only hope. I will help you all I can...and my friends will, too. But you have to find the three women, Derrick. The answer lies within two of those women. You must find that answer if your world is to survive and not be taken over by the little people."

Mallow looked at Speaks and then at the picture on the table. He thought for a minute and said, "What do I have to do, and where do I start?"

"From the beginning, Derrick, from the beginning," Speaks said while holding his head down. Because tears were filling his eyes, he was sad about the friends and relatives he lost in the battles against the little people. One of those relatives was his son.

"What's the matter, Speaks?"

"I was just thinking about those we lost in the battles against the little people."

"You want to talk about it?" Mallow asked.

"Not now, I am not ready to discuss it with anyone…*yet*," Speaks replied, raising his head and looking straight ahead.

"Speaks, may I ask what beginning you are talking about?"

"Yes."

"The beginning is when the little people first came here to your world. A long time ago, they used the lakes and rivers to set up their operations. Where they performed experiments on men, women, and children of your world. And here in Lake Tisdale is where something went 'bad wrong,'" Speaks told Mallow as he stood up and walked over to his bird cage. He touched it, rubbed the soft blanket inside, and started crying.

Speaks held his head down with his arms behind his back. He sniffled, sighed, and turned around and said, "You must eat and get some rest, Mallow. You have been through a lot. Tomorrow morning, you will start on your task to find Greta, Lucinda, and Gail."

"Are you coming with me, Speaks?" Mallow asked as he rose from the recliner and started walking to the kitchen.

"Of course, I am coming with you. But not in this form. I will be the bird again," Speaks answered quickly as he followed Mallow to the kitchen.

"You know, Mallow, I do eat people's food, too. I would love some grilled chicken, rice, and gravy," Speaks said, licking his blue tongue as Mallow smiled at him.

"Okay, Speaks. Grilled chicken and rice and gravy coming up," Mallow said as he took out two frozen dinners from the refrigerator freezer.

Speaks looked at Mallow with a frown, disappointed, and said, "I thought you were going to cook it."

"Ha! Ha! I am going to cook 'em, Speaks, in the microwave. We have to eat and get some rest like you said because tomorrow is going to come quickly. Who knows what will happen," Mallow said as he prepared the two frozen dinners for the microwave.

Speaks pulled out a chair from the kitchen table, sat down, crossed his arms, and put them on the tabletop. Then he looked out the kitchen window and said in a disconsolate tone, "Great!"

The mist encircles the SUV that Lonnie Moses is driving with Lucinda, Greta, and Gail in the back seats. Moses is in a daze, but the women are slowly awakening.

The headlights from the black king cab pickup truck shine brightly through the SUV and blind the three women from what is in front of the SUV.

There are several of the little people about four feet tall, dressed in white cloaks, with their big blue eyes glowing brightly, and their elongated teal green faces reflecting the light from the pickup truck.

Lucinda, Greta, and Gail are now awake and holding onto each other. Greta leans forward and taps Moses on the shoulder. Moses's head falls forward and lands on the steering wheel, causing the horn to blow violently.

"What's happening, Greta?" Lucinda and Gail shriek simultaneously while trying to shield their ears from the sound of the horn.

Greta took a deep breath, looked all around, and then she saw the two elderly men walking by the SUV to join the little people.

"I don't know, girls. I don't even know where we are. I can only see the little people and the two elderly men. God, we got to stop that...damn horn from blowing," Greta screamed as she gently pushed Moses down away from the steering wheel, silencing the horn.

From the back of the little people, the tan and black German Shepherd ran to the front and jumped up on the SUV's front bumper. The dog started barking at the three women who were frightened, holding each other, and crying. Then the dog looked back at the little people and whined softly.

A few seconds later, a large round blue light encircled the SUV. The dog jumped down from the SUV, and then the SUV with Moses, Lucinda, Greta, and Gail disappeared.

What's going to happen to the three women? What's going to happen to the small town of Lake Tisdale? What's going to happen to Feds Director Carlson, the senator, and the others at the Operations Center? Will Derrick Mallow, with Speaks's assistance, be able to find and save the women from the dangers of the little people?

Find out the answers and the conclusion in the next Derrick Mallow Mysteries Book 3 (The Missing Women) coming soon.

ABOUT THE AUTHOR

J.L. Melton (born November 18, 1954) is a retired electrician. He worked at a mill not far from his home in Timmonsville, South Carolina, for 32 years. He is 68 years old, married, with two sons, four stepsons, one stepdaughter, two granddaughters, and one step-grandson. He attended Hartsville High School in Hartsville, SC. He has a bachelor's degree in information technology from the University of Phoenix. In his retirement, J. L. and his wife enjoy fishing, taking vacations, and working around the house. He started writing in 2021 and hopes to write many books in the future. To him, writing is like learning a whole new field. You keep working at it and hope to get better.

J.L. Melton is the author of six other fiction books:

- *The Woods*
- *There's Something in the Slough*
- *Planet of Goblins, Witches, and Wizards*
- *Why Me? Why Me? He Asked!*
- *They Came In The Night*
- *The Town Of Outlaws*
- *The Demon Of The Lake Murders (Derrick Mallow Mysteries Book 1)*

To learn more about J.L. Melton and discover more Next Chapter authors, visit our website at www.nextchapter.pub.

Murdered By The Mist
ISBN: 978-4-82419-530-2

Published by
Next Chapter
2-5-6 SANNO
SANNO BRIDGE
143-0023 Ota-Ku, Tokyo
+818035793528

6th July 2024

Milton Keynes UK
Ingram Content Group UK Ltd.
UKHW040153010824
446405UK00002B/28

9 784824 195302